The Fun-Finder Book

Other books in the Young Women of Faith Library

The Lily Series

Here's Lily!
Lily Robbins, M.D. (Medical Dabbler)
Lily and the Creep
Lily's Ultimate Party
Ask Lily
Lily the Rebel
Lights, Action, Lily!
Lily Rules!
Rough & Rugged Lily
Lily Speaks!
Horse Crazy Lily
Lily's Church Camp Adventure
Lily's in London?!
Lily's Passport to Paris

Nonfiction

The Beauty Book
The Body Book
The Buddy Book
The Best Bash Book
The Blurry Rules Book
The It's MY Life Book
The Creativity Book
The Uniquely Me Book
The Year 'Round Holiday Book
The Values & Virtues Book
The Walk-the-Walk Book
NIV Young Women of Faith Bible

The Fun-Finder Book

Nancy Rue

ZONDERVAN.com/
AUTHORTRACKER
follow your favorite authors

The children's group of Zondervan

www.zonderkidz.com

The Fun-Finder Book
Copyright © 2003 by Women of Faith

Requests for information should be addressed to:
Zonderkidz, Grand Rapids, Michigan 49530

Library of Congress Cataloging-in-Publication Data

Rue, Nancy N.
        The fun-finder book : it's a God thing! / written by Nancy Rue; illustrated
by Lyn Boyer.
            p. cm. (Young women of faith library)
        ISBN 0-310-70258-5 (pbk.)
        1. Hobbies — Religious aspects — Christianity — Juvenile literature. 2. Girls —
Religious life — Juvenille literature. I. Boyer, Lyn. II. Title. III. Young women of faith.
BV4599.5.H67R84 2003
248.8'2 — dc21   2003000549

Published in association with the literary agency of Alive Communications, Inc.,
7680 Goddard Street, Suite 200, Colorado Springs, CO 80920.
www.alivecommunications.com

Editor: Barbara J. Scott
Interior design: Lyn Boyer
Cover design: Jody Langley

Printed in the United States of America

07 08 09 10 11 12 / 9 8 7 6 5 4 3

Contents

Excuse Me, But Aren't Hobbies for Nerds?

"Come to me, all you who are weary and burdened, and I will give you rest."
Matthew 11:28

When you think of hobbies, you may think of a kid poring over his stamp collection or a girl holding up the lunch line while she's looking through her change for that state quarter she's been trying to find for her display. And you may think, "Uh, no thanks—I have better things to do."

First of all, there is absolutely nothing wrong with stamp or coin collecting, and anybody who makes fun of a collector is being pretty narrow-minded. Why can't a person spend her leisure time in any healthy way she wants? It's *so* much better than vegging in front of the television 24/7!

Besides, hobbies are more than stamps and coins. Take a look at the kinds of hobbies the Girlz have found.

Reni is a **collector.** She's serious about perfecting her violin playing and making good grades. So collecting old kids' series books like Nancy Drew and the Bobbsey Twins from used bookstores and yard sales—and, of course, reading them—gives her a relaxing distraction from all the hard work she does. After all, a girl can't be intense *all* the time.

Kresha is an **observer.** Her family doesn't have a lot of money, so her hobby is watching people and collecting her observations about them in a notebook. Whenever she's in the doctor's office waiting room waiting for her mom or standing in line at the school water fountain, her eyes are watching and her brain is rolling. One of the best parts is—it costs nothing!

Suzy goes for **sports hobbies.** She plays soccer and does gymnastics as after-school activities, but her hobby is playing Ping-Pong at home. It helps her to play for fun, instead of always having to be competitive.

Zooey has discovered that she likes **outdoor hobbies.** Her creative outlet (the kind of thing we talked about in *The Creativity Book*) is scrapbooking, but her hobby is hiking, especially when she does it with friends and makes it a different adventure every time. She was surprised that she liked it so much— but now there's no stopping her! It makes her feel free and gives her energy.

And then there's **Lily.** Wouldn't you know that she wouldn't fall into a category? Like a lot of people, she has created an **unusual hobby.** Right now, she's becoming an expert on the medieval period—reading everything she can get her hands on, building a model of a medieval castle, designing her own medieval costumes. Once she masters that era, she might move on to the

Renaissance, or she might decide to become an expert on a particular artist, like Picasso, or read all the books written by a certain author. After all, she points out, the possibilities are endless!

So what *is* a **hobby,** exactly?

- It's an activity you do in your spare time. (Your math class can't be your hobby—like you'd *want* it to be, right?)
- It's something you enjoy doing.
- It's something you do just for fun.
- It's something you find relaxing (rather than something that complicates your life and freaks you out more!).
- It's something you see as a change from the routine of your day (no one's supervising you, no one's telling you you're doing it wrong, there are no rules, that kind of thing).

Besides the fact that a hobby is fun, it can do a lot for you.

- It can lighten you up if you tend to be hard-driving and serious about your schoolwork and other activities.
- It can expand some talents you didn't even know you had—like your eye for details or your knack for organizing.
- It can keep you from making everything a competition (because not everything is!).
- It can let you discover things you never really thought you'd enjoy because you didn't think you were good at them (and you don't have to be!).
- It can challenge your mind in fun ways. You'll probably even start doing better in school as a result of being involved in some hobby.

HOW IS this a GOD THING?

Usually when we're thinking about how something is a God thing, we go straight to the Bible. But that plan isn't so easy this time, and here's why.

Until at least the late 1800s—which is not so very long ago in the grand scheme of things—only rich people had leisure time. Most of the biblical characters sure didn't—they were too busy growing food, making cloth for clothes, carrying water, and doing everything else they had to do to survive. Without all the conveniences we have, like microwaves, washing machines and dryers, and cars, they had to do everything from scratch, and that barely left them time to sleep, let alone collect stamps — which they didn't have anyway.

So the Bible doesn't tell us anything in particular about hobbies. In fact, there are plenty of verses that speak out against idleness. When those verses were written, it was practically a crime if you weren't working dawn to dusk. Just take a look at these Proverbs!

As a door turns on its hinges, so a sluggard turns on his bed.
Proverbs 26:14

A little sleep, a little slumber,
a little folding of the hands to rest — and poverty will
come on you like a bandit and scarcity like an armed man.
Proverbs 6:10–11

He who gathers crops in summer is a wise son,
but he who sleeps during harvest is a disgraceful son.
Proverbs 10:5

Does that mean we should be working our little selves every minute, so that we don't have time for hobbies? Nah. As we've said, the folks in the Bible lived in a time when they *had* to work constantly just to survive. Only those who were wealthy and had servants could afford to indulge in hobbies. The ones in that group that God seemed to smile on were those who used their leisure time activities for his glory. That would mean that he wasn't too crazy about Herod's hobby of collecting dancing girls. But David was another story.

Harp playing was definitely a hobby for David, even when he was a kid. It was something he did while he was tending sheep, probably to relieve the boredom. (Tending sheep can be a real snooze!) He obviously practiced and played enough to get really good at it, because he was ready when Saul sent for him to soothe away his evil spirits. Later, when he was king, David celebrated the arrival of the ark of the covenant in Jerusalem by jamming on his harp. He probably also had the harp on hand when he sang his song of praise to the Lord in 2 Samuel 22:2–51.

David was also a poet. He had enough leisure time to develop that hobby, and you can read his work in 2 Samuel 1:19–27 and in many of the psalms.

Even reading one psalm shows that not only did David enjoy his hobbies—can't you see him setting some of them to music?—but he also used them to glorify God. That kind of thing definitely makes God happy. Does that mean if you have a hobby it has to be directly connected to God? Yes—but don't worry about that, because all good things are already connected to God! "Everything God created is good," Paul writes in his letter to Timothy, "and nothing is to be rejected if it is received with thanksgiving" (1 Timothy 4:4).

If you follow the example of Jesus, you can't go wrong. Though he didn't have hobbies (he, unlike you, didn't have time), he did often go off by himself to get refreshed for his demanding schedule. (If you want to see an example, you can go to Matthew 14:23.) Do the same—and use some of that time for things you enjoy that are going to help you become the person God intends for you to be.

Something a Little Different

That's probably as much as the Bible tells us about hobby time, so in the following chapters, you won't see the "It's a God Thing" section. But we will definitely be looking to God for guidance along the way—always, right?

✓ Check Yourself Out

Okay, so how do you pick a hobby that's going to be a God thing for you? It helps to start by taking a good look and deciding what things you need to develop in yourself. Let's use this quiz as our mirror.

In each of the following, circle the letter of the response that sounds most like you. Have fun with this—and be honest.

1. When it comes to school:

   a. _____ If I don't get my schoolwork done on time, I freak out or stay up half the night trying to catch up, because I must make A's!

   b. _____ I give it my best shot, and then I don't worry about it.

   c. _____ Are you kidding? I never get all my schoolwork done on time. Am I supposed to?

2. I think:

   a. _____ I have about as much talent as a dial tone; I have none!

   b. _____ I have at least one talent that I'm trying to develop.

   c. _____ I have a lot of different talents. That isn't bragging—I enjoy them, and I thank God for them!

3. When it comes to competing in things like sports or spelling competitions:

   a. _____ I go after them like a mad dog; I hate to lose.

   b. _____ I like to win, but it's not a huge deal if I don't.

   c. _____ I don't like to compete, so I stay away from that kind of stuff.

4. When I do a project:

   a. _____ I always want every detail perfect; I might even get freaked if it isn't.

b. _____ I like to do the best job I can, and if it isn't perfect I can deal with that.

c. _____ I pretty much hate it because projects are a lot of work.

5. When I'm learning about a new topic in school:

a. _____ I get bored a lot because it seems too easy. In fact, a lot of things about schoolwork are too easy for me.

b. _____ I usually learn what I'm supposed to for the tests and projects, and I'm fine with that.

c. _____ I sometimes hate it because it's way hard for me.

6. On weekends:

a. _____ I like to lie around on the couch and watch movies or TV.

b. _____ I like to do some stuff—like hobbies—and veg some.

c. _____ I like to be doing something active every minute of my free time.

Time to score! Remember that there are no right or wrong answers. What you've circled will be a big help to you as you choose a hobby that's going to be the most fun and give you the most benefits.

If you circled letter A for #1, you'll want to choose a hobby that is fun and doesn't require studying or mental work. You'll want to look at the **observing hobbies** we'll be talking about, as well as **outdoor hobbies** and **sports hobbies**. Try to avoid things like specializing in the Civil War or

collecting rare stamps—unless you can do them without being serious and intense. We're hoping you'll find a hobby that will lighten you up and let you relax more.

If you circled letter A for #2, you'll need to look at a hobby that includes something that you're really good at. You might have to try some things before you find just the right one. For example, Kresha didn't think she had any talents at all—

bless her heart—until she discovered people-watching and decided to try it. She found out she had a keen eye for details and a gift for organizing information (in her notebook). Any type of hobby will do for you as long as it starts with something you're good at. You're going to discover that you *do* have talent, and then the hobby world is going to open up for you.

If you circled letter B for #3, you'll want to choose a hobby that you do by yourself or doesn't involve winning or losing. Take a look at the **collecting hobbies,** the **observing hobbies,** the **sports hobbies that don't really seem like sports,** and **the unusual hobbies.** Those can help you keep competition from being in absolutely everything you do. It has its place, but that place isn't everywhere.

If you circled letter A for #4, you really like to do things perfectly, and that can't always happen. In order for you to find joy in something you don't have to be perfect at, look closely at **observing hobbies, outdoor hobbies,** and **unusual hobbies.** This fun stuff can help de-stress your life and teach you that you don't have to—and can't possibly be—perfect all the time.

If you circled letter A for #5, it sounds like your mind needs a challenge. To stimulate those bored brain cells, try **collecting hobbies** or **unusual hobbies.** Trying some of those can even help make school activities less boring for you.

If you circled letter A for #6, you drift toward couch potato status. Sometimes it's good to just veg, but not all your leisure time should be spent that way. You won't grow much as a person with a steady diet of sofa, soda, and sitcoms! Try **outdoor hobbies** or **sports hobbies that don't really seem like sports** for starters. They'll definitely get your blood circulating!

If you didn't circle any A's and had mostly B's, choose whatever hobby strikes your fancy. You're pretty balanced, so enjoy and watch yourself grow.

If you didn't circle any A's and had mostly C's, use the following guide:

C on #1 means you need something to get you going. Try **outdoor hobbies** or **sports hobbies that don't really seem like sports** to start with. They'll be fun and will get your mind sparking.

C on #2 means you'll have a blast turning one of your talents into a hobby. For instance, if you're a talented musician, you can learn about the lives of famous musicians—and be inspired!

C on #3 means you might be missing out on some fun stuff because you don't think you're good enough. So try a hobby that you don't have to be good at, and make sure it includes at least one other person. **Outdoor hobbies** and **sports hobbies that don't really seem like sports** would be wonderful for you.

C on #4 or #5 means you just need to find some joy in accomplishing something. That something should be a fun thing, so you might try the **observing hobbies,** the **outdoor hobbies,** and the **sports hobbies that don't seem like hobbies.** Let's get a feeling of I-can-do-it back into your life.

C on #6 means you'll want to choose a hobby that will slow you down just a little bit so you can savor what you're doing. Try **collecting hobbies** or an **unusual hobby.**

Of course we're going to show you lots of examples of these various hobbies. You'll notice as you go that we don't talk about creative hobbies—things like painting, writing, or sewing. That's because we covered those in *The Creativity Book.* If those are your thing, *this* book can still help you by giving you other options that will sort of round you out as a person. You'll also want to pay special attention to the **unusual hobbies.** Those are right up your alley!

Just Do It!

Now that you know which kinds of hobbies might be fun for you, let's take a look at some of your options. Put a star by each of the hobbies on the next pages that really attracts your attention. For now, try to stay within the categories suggested for you personally in the quiz scoring. Your choice doesn't have to be final—eventually, you can pick any hobby you want. Just work with us here for the time being!

Observing Hobbies

____ people	____ fish
____ birds	____ squirrels
____ clouds	____ bizarre hairstyles
____ wildlife	____ stars

____ people in various professions

____ the different ways people talk

or write in your own idea: _____

Collecting Hobbies

____ coins	____ stamps
____ rocks	____ buttons
____ shells	____ flowers to press
____ bugs	____ autographs
____ postcards	____ matchbooks (minus the matches)

or write in your own idea: _____

Outdoor Hobbies

____ backyard camping	____ fishing
____ hiking	____ bicycle riding
____ adventure walking	____ butterfly hunting
____ swimming for fun	____ horseback riding
____ roller-blading	____ crabbing/clam digging
____ sledding	____ gardening

or write in your own idea: _____

Sports Hobbies That Don't Really Seem Like Sports

_____ ping-pong   _____ frisbee

_____ chess   _____ backgammon

_____ swimming   _____ roller-skating

_____ ice-skating   _____ diving (at a nearby pool)

or write in your own idea:_____

Unusual Hobbies

_____   armchair traveling

_____   reading all the books by an author

_____   becoming an expert on a painter

_____   becoming an expert on a musician

_____   becoming an expert on a historical period

_____   becoming an expert on an animal species

_____   visiting old homes (because your family travels a lot)

_____   becoming an expert on weather

or write in your own (unusual) idea: _____

Now choose _one_ of the hobbies that pulled you in and write it here:

_____.

If you didn't find any of them to be your kind of thing, write down the one that sounds even a little bit interesting. You don't have to stick with it forever, but you might be surprised where it could lead once you've done this exercise.

Make one baby step in getting started on that hobby. Don't spend any money or make a huge time commitment. Just do one small thing that will get you moving toward that hobby. Here are some examples to help you:

- Pressing flowers: Take a walk around the neighborhood and check out how many wildflowers you see; maybe you'll want to write down the locations in a notebook. (Sorry—you can't pluck blossoms from people's gardens!)
- Observing people in various professions. Make a list of all the adults you know who have interesting occupations.
- Backyard camping. Scope out the garage or attic or basement for camping equipment that might be lying around and is never used anymore.
- Roller-skating. Check out the prices at the local skating rink.
- Becoming an expert on snow leopards. Dig out those National Geographic magazines that are stacked in the basement and look through them for snow leopard articles or take a trip to the library.

Write your baby step plan here—and then, just do it! _____

_____

GIRLZ want to know

Because you still live under your parents' roof—and because, let's face it, you're still a kid—your hobby choices are sometimes limited by house rules. The Girlz had some questions about how to handle that. Maybe our answers will help you too.

❀ *KRESHA: I have so many hobbies I want to get into, but we don't have much money for extra stuff at my house. I know if I even ask my mother to pay for hobby equipment, she'll ground me! Can I still have a hobby?*

Of course you can! In fact, the less money you spend on a hobby, the more creative it is and the better it works in helping you grow as a person. Almost every hobby we've listed can be done without putting out cash. Here are some suggestions.

- Let people know what hobby you'd like to pursue and that new equipment is out of the question. Some used equipment might almost magically emerge from somebody's garage.

- Try to make some money—maybe walking people's dogs or pulling weeds—and then use your saved-up cash to visit yard sales for the things you need. Just be sure any sports equipment is still safe to use.

- Make sure you really need what you think you need. Do you have to have a new notebook to write down your observations, or could you make one from binder paper and a cover you make yourself?

- If none of that works, choose a hobby that doesn't require anything but you and your imagination. Look back through the list and look for those kinds of hobbies—they're fun!

✿ *RENI: I like my hobby, but sometimes I get so busy with school and violin lessons and school orchestra and all-city orchestra and youth group at church, I don't get to play around with it as often as I want to. But I can't drop any of that other stuff, so what should I do?*

Life can definitely get hectic sometimes—and the whole purpose of hobbies is to distract us from our demanding schedules from time to time so we can relax and get refueled for the next round. It's a good idea, then, to plan time for your hobby just like you plan time for everything else. Here are some ideas for doing that.

- Pick a realistic goal for how often you'd like to spend time on your hobby—once a week? Every other week?

- Then write all your other activities on a calendar. Be sure to write down how long each one takes (example: violin lesson 3:20–4:20).

- Look carefully for spaces in your schedule. What about Saturday morning when you'd usually be sleeping in until noon or watching cartoons in a stupor? Or during those weekly hour-long rides to your grandmother's house? You'll be surprised where you can find blocks of time you never knew you had.

- Now write time for your hobby on the calendar in one of those spaces. Stick to that date and time just as you would to your violin lessons or your orchestra rehearsal. Be sure you aren't putting more stress on yourself when trying to keep your dates with your hobby. If it doesn't work out one week, don't try to cram it in there anyway—it will still be there next week, and you won't be too stressed out to enjoy it!

❁ *ZOOEY: I love coming home from backpacking with my friends and writing all about it in my journal and drawing pictures of what I've seen. But do I get the peace and quiet to do that? How 'bout no! First it's my brother poking his head in and saying, "What are you doing, weirdo?" Then my mother wants to know why I have my door closed. Plus—I know my mom has looked in my journal when I'm not home. How can I get some privacy so I can enjoy my hobby? Is it bad to want that?*

It's not bad to want privacy. It's normal for a girl your age to want some time and space alone, especially when it's to pursue a hobby. But that sudden need for privacy—when you probably used to be in your mom's face all the time when you were a little kid—can be hard for your mom to understand at first. It may seem to her that if you don't have anything to hide, you shouldn't need privacy. These days, a lot of parents are worried about things like drugs, which are available to younger and younger kids all the time. Maybe you can help your mom by using these suggestions.

- Share what you're doing with your hobby with your mom one day—especially your journal.

- Explain to her (in your calmest, most mature voice) why you like to be by yourself without interruptions when you're drawing pictures and recording your experiences.

- Ask her if you can have at least an hour every time you come back from backpacking to gather your thoughts with the door closed.

If you do that, chances are your mother will let you have your privacy, at least for the time you've asked, because she now has no reason to worry. She might even help you out with that brother of yours!

LILY: *I'm getting along with my brothers better all the time, but my younger brother still thinks it's weird that I like to study medieval fashions and draw my own costumes instead of playing volleyball. And he's not the only one. I have to be really careful who I tell at school. All I need is for Ashley and her group to get wind of what I do in my spare time and I'll be the laughing stock of the whole place. I feel like I either have to do it all in secret (like up in the attic, wearing a disguise!) or just give it up and be like everybody else.*

No way, Lily! Never settle for being like everybody else. You're unique—a real individual—and if you've found a part of your uniqueness, you go with it! But it's *so* normal at this point in your life to want to be accepted for who you are. When you aren't accepted, it's also normal for it to hurt. But these suggestions will help you deal with ridicule.

- Ask your parents to help you out in the brother department. They'll probably do what they can, and then it will be up to you to ask him, as nicely as possible, to knock it off. After that—ignore, ignore, ignore. It's tough, but the more you respond, the worse it's going to get. (That's the way little brothers operate!)

- Follow your instinct to keep your hobby among your closest friends. Why open yourself up to teasing?

- At the same time, don't try to be like them just to be accepted. That will erase all the good things your hobby is doing for you.

Talking To God About It

Dear _____, (your favorite way of addressing God)
Thank you for creating me at a time in history when we have leisure time for hobbies, and thank you for all the good things a hobby can do for me. Now I have some things to ask you, and I pray that you'll answer with whatever is your will.

When it comes to choosing a hobby, would you help me

_____
_____
_____?

When it comes to getting started on my hobby, I need help with

_____
_____
_____.

There are some roadblocks to my really enjoying my hobby, like

_____
_____
_____.

By getting into this hobby, Father, I hope to develop

_____
_____.

Would you help me with those, and will you let me know if I'm heading in the right direction?

I want to live the abundant life you want me to live. Thank you for making it possible.

I love you!

Lily Pad

If I could choose any hobby, it would be ...

The Complete Collection

Store up for yourselves treasures in heaven.
Matthew 6:20

When people think of hobbies, collections are the first thing that pops into their minds, so if the results of your quiz told you that a **collecting hobby** might be fun for you, you're not alone!

It was natural for **Reni** to choose a collecting hobby (remember her collection of old book series like Nancy Drew?). From the time she was a little kid, she was always dragging home stuff for her huge collection of collections — bottles, buttons, rocks, shells, pieces of broken colored glass (her mom put the kibosh on that last one — and come to think of it, Mom wasn't too crazy about the bug collection, either!).

As she got older, she narrowed down the number of collections (it was either that or move into a bigger room) and got a little more sophisticated with the ones she did have. She no longer stored her rocks in a Tupperware container, but graduated to a piece of plywood her dad cut for her. She glued each rock onto it and labeled it with where she found it. The shells went on a shelf with tags attached. The buttons she pasted into a scrapbook with notes written under each. She became more selective about her collectibles, picking up only the best-looking rocks, the most unusual buttons, and shells that were all in one piece.

Now that Reni's even older and has a brand-new collection, she has a box of note cards with comments about each book she's found and read. People know she's a collector. So when they come across articles or books about the things she's interested in, they give them to her. She set up a corner of her room with bookshelves where she houses her collection, and there's a nearby stack of floor pillows so she can curl up and read and reread (and sometimes even re-reread).

Hopefully, this sounds fun and you're inspired to come up with your own collection. But you may be thinking, "How did Reni get such a cool idea? How am I gonna figure out something that neat? And once I do, how will I get organized?"

Why don't we stop here and look first at the question of how to get an idea? Then we'll fill you in on how to get organized and on all the answers to those other questions that are waving their arms in your head, waiting to be called on.

✓ Check Yourself Out

The best way to think of a collection idea is to, once again, look into your self-mirror and find out what would make the perfect collection for you. Before we start, remember this guideline—nothing you come up with is nerdy or stupid or lame or weird.

Read each of the following short sections and draw a star next to each section that sparks an idea. There's a space provided at the end of each for you to jot down those new thoughts if you want to. You'll probably want to capture them before they flit away.

NATURE

Collecting things from God's creation involves being outside a lot, keeping a sharp eye out for the best specimens. You stroll along a beach, looking for seashells tucked into the sand, or run across a sunny field with your butterfly net flowing in the breeze over your shoulder. You might hike in the hills, poking around for the coolest rocks and probably stopping for a picnic. Or you could kick around in the woods, spotting just the right leaves in the dappling of sunlight. Maybe you could settle in on your back porch on a summer's evening, ready to nab that insect you've been on the lookout for. Or you might take walks anywhere and spot a flower you don't already have, poking up through a crack in the sidewalk.

Your ideas: _____

Antique

We're not talking about going into an expensive antique shop and purchasing a hanky for $150! There are plenty of old things that are free if you keep your eyes open and put out the word.

Having an antique collection will mean liking history more and appreciating all those people who have gone before you. You get to spend hours at your grandmother's, going through her box of old photographs, or afternoons sitting on the deck with your great-grandfather, writing down all the funny old stories he tells you. Or you might go to yard sales on Saturdays, digging through the merchandise for old buttons, road maps, salt and pepper shakers, and then parting with some of your allowance. Or on a rainy evening, you might spend some time organizing the old things people give you once they know you are a collector and appreciate old stuff—journals, postcards, greeting cards, for example.

Your ideas: _____

If you like to read, which means you like words, this kind of collection might do it for you. You get to pull out your special autograph book every time you meet a new person you like. Or you might spend New Year's Day delivering cookies to your neighbors and trading them for last year's calendars. Or you could curl up with a stack of newspapers and magazines with scissors in hand for cutting out only the funniest cartoons. Maybe you could eat out with your family and friends so that you can add to your menu collection or explore relatives' attics (with their permission) in search of old letters. You might look through your collection of bookmarks every time you start a new book, to choose just the right one. Or you could raid free displays at hotels and travel agencies for brochures about unusual places.

Your ideas: _____

The artist in you might enjoy collecting visual things. If you have a collection of things pictorial, you can watch for outdated posters around town and ask if you can have them for your poster collection. Or you could amuse yourself while you're waiting at doctors' offices and other businesses by picking up the neatest-looking business cards. You could spend an otherwise boring Saturday afternoon going through magazines and newspapers, looking for pictures of the people you most admire. Or you might want to save your allowance for that new set of paper dolls you've had your eye on for your collection. It's fun to imagine you were there, as you look at programs people give you (now that they know you're a collector) from theater performances, concerts, football games, or recitals. Or you could feel like you're filling yourself up with God when you add one more Christian symbol to your already thick scrapbook.

Your ideas: _____

These better-known collections are easier to find because a lot of other people collect them too. That doesn't mean you're not original. After all, you get to pounce on the mail every day looking for unusual stamps or postmarks, or daydream as you gaze into your colorful jar of unusual marbles. You might examine the change every time you go to the store with your mom or dad, trying to find that year penny you haven't acquired yet. Or you could save your allowance for the matchbox car or piece of miniature doll furniture you want to add to the shelf or dollhouse. Another idea is to go to yard sales on Saturdays in search of frog figurines or stuff with turtles on it or anything related to ballet, or keep an eye out after elections for cast-off political buttons, pins, bumper stickers, and posters.

Your ideas: _____

If you haven't found something that makes you want to get started right away in any of the above sections, let your mind travel through this list until you find something that interests you or something that gives you an idea of your own:

badges

costume jewelry

fans

masks

beads

pennants

newspaper headlines

pincushions

thimbles

jokes

small unusual boxes

tickets

valentines

bells

unusual pencils

puzzles

matchbooks

crosses

riddles

slogans

yo-yos

Just Do It

By now, hopefully, you're completely jazzed and are ready to get started with your collection. If you're not, read on. You will be soon! (And if you never get jazzed, maybe a collection isn't your bag. Don't despair—there are four more chapters to go!)

As you read the suggestions below for how to gather, organize, display, record, and enjoy your collection, remember that you don't have to do all these things the first week. That's the cool thing about a collection—it's something you gather over time, relishing each new item that joins the group.

We've tried to give suggestions that won't cost you money. Anything that does call for some cash is in *italics* and is optional, which means you don't have to have it. The do-it-yourself-freebie suggestions are given first each time.

Before you start bringing home your treasures, make sure of two things.

1. You have your parents' permission and are ready to observe any limits they set (such as "Wildflowers have to be pressed within twenty-four hours—no leaving dead flowers lying around for weeks.")

2. You have a place to store your items until you have a chance to record them and mount them or put them in just the right place on the shelf. It'll be most exciting for you if you do that right away, but you can't always manage it—what with chores, piano lessons, and watching your little brother. So in order to stay organized and keep peace at home, set up a storage system.

Empty plastic margarine tubs are great for that. So is an old suitcase nobody uses anymore. A big envelope is good for your paper items. Don't leave your stuff in there too long, though. If you do, it isn't a collection—it's just stuff and likely to get thrown away in the next big cleaning!

• At your next opportunity, start collecting. At first you might have the urge to snatch up anything that's even remotely related to your collection, but try to curb that urge. Pick only the best examples of what you're looking for. Keep in mind that a collection isn't about how many items you have, but how special each item is. Four perfect seashells are definitely a better collection than a bag of broken pieces.

• Between collecting times, or even before your first one, decide how you're going to organize your collection. How will you keep track of where and when you got each piece? What is its history (if that makes sense for your type of collection)? What is its correct name (in the case of rocks, shells, butterflies, leaves, that kind of thing)? You might want to keep a written record in a notebook, with numbers to correspond with the numbers you put on stickers on each item. You can hang tags on your items or write under them if you display them on a board or in a scrapbook. A card file is also a neat way. You can make small cards out of paper and find a box they'll fit into, *or you can buy a small file box and a package of index cards.*

The idea is to be able to look at your record at any time and know exactly what each item is, where it came from, when you got it, and any other fun and interesting information. Don't forget to include your experience in making each little treasure your own, if that sounds like fun to you. None of these are have-tos. You can keep your marbles in a jar and let it go at that. But you'll probably find this to be a lot more fun, and you'll learn tons without even realizing it!

- Decide before you get too many items collected how you're going to display your collection. That doesn't mean it has to be out for the whole world to see all the time. But it's fun to have it ready to pull out and show to people who think you're fascinating because you collect unusual barrettes, clips, and scrunchies.

  The way you display your collection depends on the collection. If there's a book in your library about your type of collection—as there will be for things like stamps, coins, pressed flowers, and leaves—check it out and see what suggestions are given that you could follow with items you already have. For those kinds of collections, *you can also go to a hobby shop and buy albums, display cases, and shelves.* For the less-than-usual hobby collection, you'll probably have to decide on your own, maybe with the help of a grown-up, especially somebody you know who collects things. We can't cover absolutely every kind of collection here, but we can give you some general pointers.

1. **Scrapbooks**—perfect for things like newspaper clippings and pictures. If you think you're going to keep your collection for a long time,

ask for acid-free paper and acid-free glue on your next birthday or for Christmas. Avoid using tape or staples or albums with those plastic sticky sheets, because those will eventually ruin your stuff.

2. **Walls** — things like calendars and posters can be mounted on your bedroom wall, if that's okay with your folks.

3. **Poster board and plywood** — you may have poster board around the house or plywood that's been sitting in the garage forever and no one's ever going to use it. These make great display boards for things like shells and rocks, buttons, political buttons, or anything small that can be mounted. *You can also buy pegboard and little hooks at a hardware store.*

4. **Egg cartons and tackle boxes** — for small items like rocks, shells, or miniature figures, an egg carton or an old fishing tackle box can be cool display cases, especially when decorated with your own special flair.

5. **Shelves** — you won't want to keep figurine-type collections hidden away.

If you have a shelf in your room already, great — unless your mom doesn't want the dust gathering, in which case you can promise to dust them yourself weekly — oh, and keep that promise!

If you don't have a shelf, ask if you can use the top of your dresser or scrounge around in the garage or attic for one nobody's using. Should that fail, you can make a display case out of a really sturdy cardboard or wood box. The best kind of box is the kind bottled beverages come in because it already has dividers. Ask about those at your grocery store. If Mom wants you to keep your collection in your closet, that's okay. You'll be ready to pull it out if someone shows the slightest interest in seeing it!

• Take really good care of your collection. It's going to need some upkeep. Once again, special books on stamp or coin collecting or pressing flowers and leaves will be in your library. So will books that help you identify rocks, butterflies, or shells. Those books will tell you how to take care of particular kinds of collectibles. For others, like figurines, dust them at least once a week, and when it becomes hard to get the dust off—they feel sticky—wash them with soap and water. (This is only if your figurines are washable. This won't work for paper dolls!)

- If you've been collecting for a while and you're ready to move on to something else, you may not want to save what you have. See if there is someone else who would like to have some or all of your stuff. This is especially true with things like coins, stamps, and marbles. Don't forget to ask your younger sibling(s), who may be thrilled to have that collection of pig figurines.

- Remember as you're doing all this that it's supposed to be something you enjoy. If at any time it becomes a chore or you find yourself getting frustrated because it isn't all coming out perfectly, take a break from it for a while or go back and remember why you started your collection. You may need to lighten up or move on to another hobby. You haven't spent much money, if any, so it's okay to let it go. A hobby should never be a have-to kind of thing.

GIRLZ want to know

✿ *ZOOEY: I already go hiking as my hobby, but now I want to start collecting neat things I find along the way, like leaves and rocks and stuff. The problem is that I just know my mom is going to flip because she'll be afraid I'll bring dirt in the house.*

Easy fix! Decide that you're going to be responsible about this and always clean your collected items before you bring them into the house. Decide that you'll do it right away, as soon as you get home. That way you won't clutter up the back porch or the garage for more than a minute. Get your storage system all ready (plastic margarine tubs, etc.).

The next time you go hiking, select one item, bring it home, clean it outside, and show it to your mom. Explain to her how you've handled it and what you'd like to do with the pieces you bring home. Produce that storage system. Show that you're responsible. She's bound to say it's okay or at least say okay with some limits. Respect those limits—to the limit! If it doesn't work out, you might ask if you can keep your collection in the garage. But don't wheedle. You might have to settle for drawing or writing about the things you see on your hikes, but that really wouldn't be so bad.

✿ *LILY: Okay—since I'm already doing my medieval period hobby, I could combine it with collecting those greeting cards that have medieval pictures on them. They aren't expensive, so I could use my chore money, and my mom already said I could tack them on my walls. The problem is—why does there always have to be a problem? I can't get to the shops where they sell those kinds of cards that often. It's not like I can drive there myself! My parents are way busy, and I can't even imagine my brother taking me and hanging around with all that foo-foo stuff. I'm all set, except for that.*

Yes, there is always a problem—but there is always a solution too. You could squirrel your money away until the next opportunity comes up, but that probably isn't the best answer you've ever heard. Here are a few suggestions for getting where you need to go for your hobby.

- Use some of that saved-up money to buy your brother a Coke and a burger if he'll take you sometime soon. Promise to be in the store only twenty minutes max — and in return for that, do twenty minutes of his chores. Look for other incentives — is there a nice girl working in the store he could talk to while you're shopping? Is there a music store near your card shop or on the way (since we know he does the music thing) that you would agree to hang out in while *he* shops? This isn't bribery — it's just making it worth his while!

- If you get to have alone time with your dad, mom, or both, ask if a trip to the card shop can be included next time. Then leave it alone. Nagging will get you nowhere!

- When a relative in town asks what you'd like for Christmas or a birthday, suggest a ride to the card shop. That person doesn't even have to buy you anything — you just want to get there!

- If your parents give rewards for things like good grades, ask that instead of cash or a trip out for ice cream, they take you to the card store for thirty minutes. Again, they don't have to buy anything for you — you've got that handled!

- If none of that gets you where you want to go as often as you'd like, make it known that you like those cards. Chances are, you'll start receiving them for your birthday or on just-because occasions. They may not be the ones you would have chosen, but you never know — your eyes might be opened to new possibilities.

✿ *KRESHA: I think I want to collect unusual pictures of ordinary people from magazines to go along with my observing-people hobby. I already know I want to make a collage as I collect them, and I already have a piece of poster board from school that was used on only one side, and my mom got me some glue. I have an old school folder I'm going to keep the pictures in until I have a chance to put them on the collage. But — and this is a big but—I have two younger brothers. As soon as they find out I have anything they don't have, they'll be in my room so fast! How can I keep their sticky little hands off of my glue and pictures and stuff?*

Little brothers, lovable as they can be at times, can also be like the plague. But there is now a cure for that plague. Try these suggestions:

- Talk to your mom about letting you keep your supplies and collected pictures in her room. Chances are they don't raid that space too often!

- Ask one of your friends if you can keep it in her closet. Maybe the two of you could pursue that hobby together, which might be even more fun.

- Ask your mom if she can pick up a couple of inexpensive containers of glue for your little brothers—or when you see some running out at school, ask the teacher if you can take them home. Set up your brothers at the kitchen table (with your mom's permission). Give them their glue and some of your cast-off magazines and a piece of paper each or some more of that old poster board. Help them make their own collages and then show them yours. They don't have to know that you have a different kind of special glue—that isn't lying, that's protecting your property. Once they feel like they get to have this stuff too, they'll probably back off of yours. Just in case, keep it as hidden as you can.

Talking To God About It

In this prayer to God, concentrate on the areas that apply to you.

Dear _____, (your favorite way of addressing our Father)

I'm really excited about starting my collection. Please help me not let this become too much about collecting things and more about seeing you in the new world I'll be discovering. I'm a little concerned about _____, so could you help me out with that?

I want to do a collection, but none of the ideas I've heard about appeals to me, and I feel stupid and lame or lazy and dumb. Could you help me deal with my feelings of _____? Could you help me find something I'll enjoy—something in the area of _____ _____or steer me in another direction?

Please help me to remember that this hobby is supposed to bring me closer to you and help me learn more about myself.

I sure love you!

Lily Pad

If I could do a God collection, I would collect...

According to My Observations

**Listen to this ... stop and consider
God's wonders.**
Job 37:14

Kresha took up people-watching as a hobby partly because it costs her nothing. But it wasn't like she said to herself, "I need a hobby. I think I'll pick a cheap one."

It happened more like this.

One day she had to sit in the dentist's office almost a whole afternoon while her mom and her two little brothers had their teeth cleaned and cavities filled. At first she was practically bored into a stupor, until she noticed a man sitting across from her. He was holding a magazine and appeared to be reading it — except that he was holding it upside down. And as Kresha sneaked a closer look, that wasn't the only thing odd about him. The curly-headed man was wearing a beret, cocked jauntily to the side of his head. He had one of those moustaches that curl up at the ends, and the frames of his glasses were bright red.

When he caught her watching him, Kresha looked away, but she couldn't get him out of her mind. She really wanted to tell the Girlz about him the next day, but she was afraid she'd forget the details. So she dug into her backpack for one of her school notebooks — the one for art class that she'd never written anything in — and jotted it all down. Then she couldn't help herself — she did a drawing too.

When the man went in for his appointment, Kresha looked around the room with new eyes. She spotted a child staring into the fish tank, picking his nose; an elderly woman with almost blue hair whose perfume filled the waiting room, and a teenage girl with the longest fingernails she'd ever seen, listening to an iPod and swinging her unruly head of permed hair from side to side. Kresha also saw a woman sitting quietly in the corner. She too held a magazine, but Kresha could tell she wasn't really reading it. It was more as if she were hiding behind it, so no one could see her very sad face.

Before Kresha knew it, she was scribbling madly. The time flew by, and when her mom and brothers came out, she was almost disappointed that her wait was over.

It wasn't until that same sort of thing happened later that week while she was standing in line with her mom at the post office, and then several days later when she finished a test early and had to sit quietly in her seat, that Kresha began to see that a habit was forming — a habit she liked — a habit that was fun (as opposed to brushing her teeth and picking up her dirty clothes). She decided to keep it up, collecting her observations in her notebook, which she decorated just for that purpose, and including the occasional drawing. It's a great hobby, because it does several things for her.

- It opens her eyes to the world around her.
- It makes her aware of how different people can be.
- It makes her feel more like a part of the human family.
- It sharpens her powers of observation.
- It makes her pay more attention to detail.
- It helps her become more organized.

Most of the time, that's what an **observing hobby** can do for you. And usually, as in Kresha's case, it's the kind of thing that finds *you,* rather than you having to go out looking for it. It's a matter of taking a deeper view of what you're already looking at.

✓ Check Yourself Out

Let's give your observing hobby a chance to find you.

Wherever you are right now as you're reading this book—in your room, in a car, up in a tree, at your desk at school, wherever—casually glance around. Write down the first three things you notice, without really thinking about it too much. What three things catch your eye first?

1. _____
2. _____
3. _____

Look again, a little more closely this time. Write down three things you'd like to look at some more—maybe even stare at and study. They can be some or all the same things you wrote in the first part if that's what's happened.

1. _____
2. _____
3. _____

Put the items from both sections in their matching columns below:

THINGS ABOUT NATURE

1. _____

2. _____

3. _____

4. _____

Things About Manmade Stuff

1. _____

2. _____

3. _____

4. _____

THINGS ABOUT PEOPLE

1. _____

2. _____

3. _____

4. _____

If you want to, continue this quiz in other places over the next day or two. When you're finished, count how many of your most-interesting-to-you observations have fallen in each category and write the numbers below:

- Things From Nature_____
- Things About People_____
- Things About Manmade Stuff (Like Art or Clothes)_____

Time to score. This is the least like scoring of any quiz we've done yet— but it will tell us some things. (You may have a balance of observations in all three categories or maybe two, which is fine. That means you'll feel comfortable picking from both or all of those areas under "Just Do It" below.)

If most of your observations were in the "people" category, chances are you'd have fun observing some of these things:

- the different ways people talk
- hairstyles
- the different ways people walk
- people and their dogs
- the different things people like to eat
- how guys are different from girls
- the different ways people express their emotions
- how different families do the family thing
- the different cliques at school
- the different types of careers people choose
- babies
- older people

If most of your observations were in the "nature" category, you might enjoy observing some of these things:

- dogs
- cats
- frogs
- birds
- fish
- sunsets
- weather
- trees
- clouds
- wild animals
- lizards
- turtles
- insects
- flowers
- rock formations
- stars

If most of your observations were in the "manmade stuff" category, it's a good bet you'd like observing some of these things:

- paintings and drawings
- sculpture
- architecture
- furniture
- clothes
- costumes
- jewelry
- cars
- construction work
- music (which you'll observe with your ears)

As always, you don't *have* to stick with the observing hobby that seems to have discovered you at this point. Pick whatever you want, or combine some of the above. If none of those things do it for you, read on. You might get inspired, or you may want to move on to another chapter. There are three more after this one — and everybody will probably read all of them anyway, because you never know what might wave its hand at you and say, "Take me! Take me!"

Just Do It!

As you read the suggestions below for how to set yourself up and observe and record and enjoy, keep reminding yourself that it isn't all going to happen at once. That's one of the best things about an observing hobby — it can go on for as long as you want it to. There are no deadlines, and you can savor every experience as it happens.

As in the chapter about collections, we've tried to give suggestions that won't cost you money. Anything that does call for some cash is in *italics* and is optional, which means you don't have to have it. The do-it-yourself, freebie suggestions are given first each time.

- Before you begin, make sure that you have your parents' permission and are ready to follow any limits they set (such as "No staring at people openly in public" or "No going off on nature walks by yourself"). It may seem ridiculous to you to have to ask permission to look around, but your mom or dad may think of things that never entered your mind regarding safety and manners. Not that you're a goof or anything. That's just what parents are supposed to do for you.
- Figure out how you're going to record your observations. Don't depend on your memory, or you'll forget small details. How you do that depends on what you have at home already available to you and how much detail you want to go into. Here are some guidelines:

1. If you plan to people watch wherever you go, you'll need a small notebook or pad that will fit in your backpack, pocket, or purse.

2. If you're going to do your observing only on walks or hikes or from a sitting-down place (like a bench at the zoo), a little larger size will do because you won't be constantly lugging it around.

3. If you plan to do detailed drawings or it's easier for you to write in big letters, you only need something relatively big, like a sketch pad.

4. Decide also whether you want to organize your observations (your data) as you go or do it later. If you want to organize as you go, keep reading for suggestions on how to do that. (You'll be doing it eventually, but you might want to be a little looser while you're looking.)

5. Don't forget something to write with. Pick your pen or pencil carefully, and make sure you have extras. It needs to be something you're really comfortable with—and it definitely needs to be something fun. This is the perfect time to use the purple gel pen you aren't allowed to do assignments with in school or the ballpoint with the feather on the end of it that you've been saving. Don't bother with an eraser—because nothing that you write down while you're observing has to be perfect.

It's pretty simple, really. You look and write what you see, or you listen and write what you hear, or sniff and write what you smell—you get the idea. There are a few things you might not think of, though, so look through this list of guidelines:

When people watching:

A. Don't stare openly at people. Try to be subtle about the fact that you're watching someone. You have the perfect right to do so, of course, but it isn't polite to make people feel uncomfortable.

B. Never laugh or kid around with friends you're with about what you're observing about other people.

C. Resist the urge to go up and talk to somebody who seems really interesting, unless your parents are with you and they sense that it would be okay. Even a gang of friends around you can't make it safe for you to approach strangers.

D. If you do talk to somebody, don't make it seem as if you're examining him or her like some kind of specimen. Your mom or dad can guide you on making it a friendly conversation.

E. If you want to take photographs, always ask permission of the person whose picture you want to take. It's the right thing to do. Some groups don't believe it's a good thing for them to be photographed. Don't argue the point. Just politely take no for an answer.

When nature watching:

A. If you're in a park or zoo or on private property, always ask permission, especially if you're going to try to get close to an animal or plant. Find out first what the rules and limitations are and then follow them. If the sign says stay off the grass, stay off the grass. If it says no fingers in the lion's cage, well then...

B. Before you take photographs, ask permission unless you're out in no-man's land or your own yard. Never assume that it's okay.

C. If you're observing something you're not already an expert on, it would help to have a book along that shows the names of the things you're observing. You can check out of the library any bird-watching, flower-watching, snake-watching (yikes!), and any other kind of watching books. *Or you can look for them in used bookstores or yard sales or buy them new.* It's best to have the book with you unless you're taking photographs, because once you're home, they can all begin to look the same in your head!

D. For small or faraway things like insects or birds, a pair of binoculars is nice but not absolutely necessary. If you think it would be fun to have a pair, *save your money and check out yard sales or thrift*

stores. Now, if you're really looking faraway — like at the stars — a telescope is great, but don't even think about asking your parents to buy one! (Those babies are expensive!) Instead, ask them to take you to a planetarium. There's one in every big city. If you can't make it, don't worry. Lying on your back under the stars with a constellation chart and a flashlight can be just as much fun.

When observing manmade stuff:

A. In an art gallery or any other place where art is displayed, never take photographs unless you ask permission. The people in charge will probably say no because they are protecting someone's artwork from flash damage and from being copied by some evil person. Be as quiet in a gallery as you would be in a library. Most art observers like to have silence while they're soaking it in.

B. In a museum, the same thing goes.

C. When it comes to any display or antique or specialty store where you're looking, resist the urge to touch anything unless you ask permission. You're looking at someone's collection, so it's polite to make sure it's okay. And sometimes it won't be because every human touch of something old deteriorates it just a little more.

D. Even though you're just observing, it can be tempting to pick up a souvenir, such as a fallen piece of plaster off of that old building you're looking at so carefully. It's best to just leave it there.

E. If you're observing people at work, once again, ask permission and ask questions only when there's a lull in the action so you don't hold up progress or come off as annoying.

F. If you're observing a live musical performance, don't talk — or even whisper — while the artists are playing. It's distracting and makes them think you aren't listening.

Now go for it! If you're having trouble figuring out where to find what you're looking for, read the answers to "Girlz Want to Know" below.

- Between observing times, or even before your first one, decide how you're going to permanently record your observations. How will you keep track of where and when you caught each sighting — what its history is (if that makes sense for your type of observing) — what the proper names are, in the case of birds, stars, pieces of music or art, that kind of thing? If you're recording neatly as you go (and if you are, you're amazing!), you've already taken care of this step, but if you're just jotting down notes, now's the time to make that decision.

  You might want to set up a logbook with columns for different kinds of information. Or set up a binder with different sections — so that if you're watching people in different professions, for instance, you have a different section in the binder for each type of job. Or maybe you'd prefer a scrapbook, especially if you're taking pictures or making drawings. Or perhaps you just want to write it all in story form in a journal.

  There are record books already set up for such things as bird watching and star gazing in bookstores, hobby shops, nature stores, and sports stores, and you can look through them to get ideas for your own. But don't feel as though you can't go on with your hobby if you don't have one. It's way more fun to create your own.

- Unlike collecting, this is not the kind of hobby you display. It's usually a more private thing that you enjoy yourself. If you really want to share your stuff with somebody, why not consider forming a little group of observers who come together once a week or so to tell each other what they're learning and pass around the scrapbooks and journals — and cookies! If any friend or family member is interested, by all means share away!

- Remember as you're doing all this that it's supposed to be something you enjoy. If at any time it gets boring or you've observed all you want to observe, take a break from it for a while, or start a new observing hobby, or expand this one. If you've been observing clouds, for instance, maybe you'd like to get into the whole weather thing. If you want to move on to something else, you haven't spent much money, if any, so let it go. As we've said before, a hobby should never be a have-to kind of thing.

GIRLZ want to know

The biggest question the Girlz, and maybe you, have is where to find the things they want to observe. It's one thing to watch people at airports and grocery store check-out lines or gaze at the stars from your back deck every night. It's something else to want to see professional art or watch elephants. Hopefully, our answers to them will help you as well.

✿ *RENI: I think it would be so cool to observe art to go along with my whole violin thing. It seems like they go together somehow. But where do I find real art to look at? That seems impossible!*

You're right that good music and fine art do go together, probably because the same kind of people enjoy and appreciate both of them. But you're wrong that it's impossible to find. Here are some suggestions:

- Art galleries, of course (duh!). But the one you visit doesn't have to be the Metropolitan Museum of Art in New York City. Even small towns have little art galleries tucked away, and anyone you know who is an artist of some kind or who enjoys art will be able to tell you where those secret places are. If there's a big city nearby, perhaps a trip to a gallery would be something you could request for your birthday instead of the usual cake and candles party.

- Public places. Many of them display art—airports, banks, big office buildings, and restaurants, just to name a few.

- Art books. There are sure to be some at your school and public libraries. It isn't exactly the same as seeing it for real, hanging in a frame, but if you get quiet and maybe turn on some of that music you love, you can lose yourself in a painting in a book just as easily.

- Good card stores and bookstores. They almost always have note cards with famous art reproduced on them. And while you're there, some bookstores have comfortable chairs that invite you to sit down and look at an art book, even if you don't intend to buy it. Obviously, you'd want to treat it with care and not take up space on the couch for hours!

✿ *ZOOEY: You know by now that I'm getting to be a nature freak! I think I'm really going to love watching sunsets and clouds and stuff while I'm hiking, but our Adventure Club day-long trips happen only every once in a while, and I'd like to go more often. Where else can I find nature things to observe?*

Nature is all around you all the time, except when you're cooped up indoors. Even then there are indoor plants and flowers. Try these suggestions.

- It might seem hokey, but look in your backyard! You have clouds and stars over your house. A homemade bird feeder made out of peanut butter and a pinecone will attract more birds for watching than you might think.

- Is there a local park you can go to for squirrel or pigeon-watching? (They never fail to show up!)

- Do you have a friend you can visit who lives further out of town?

- Is there a duck pond at some business or college nearby?

- If you exhaust all those opportunities and it's still two weeks 'til the next Adventure Club trip and you need your nature fix, look up nature info about the place you're going to visit. Check out what kinds of birds and wildlife and foliage you will probably see there. It's fun sometimes to finally see something you've only been looking at pictures of — and very cool to already know something about it.

❀ *SUZY: I want to observe gymnasts and divers and ice-skaters because I like the way they move. But the question is —*

Yeah, I know what the question is: Where do you find them? You might have the easiest fix of all! Try these:

- Television isn't *completely* evil! Every weekend there are competitions and shows of the kinds of things you want to watch, especially on sports channels. It's the next best thing to being there. If you don't like the commentaries, turn off the sound. If your parents limit your TV watching (good for them!), save your hours for these events. If your siblings give you grief about hogging the television, bargain with them. If all else fails, tape the program you want to watch and view it when your sisters are off doing something else.

- Save your allowance and *rent videotapes.* Most large video stores have sports sections.

- *Watch for special events coming to your area,* like ice-skating shows.

- Don't insist on professionals. Almost-professionals can be just as enjoyable to watch. Does your local college have a diving competition coming up that you can go to? Check with a nearby gymnastics gym to see when the next local competition is going to be held. If your city or town has an ice-skating rink, go and watch people practice. There are good skaters out there who just like to do it for fun and will put on a show for you without even knowing it (it's their hobby!).

Talking to God About It

Dear _____, (your favorite way of addressing God)

I never knew I could make a whole hobby out of just opening my eyes! Thanks for making it that way and for giving us so much to look at in the first place! I'm going to check off some things that I pray you'll help me with as I go:

_____ remembering to look for you in whatever I'm observing

_____ not whining when I don't get to go where I want to go for observing when I want to go there

_____ not getting upset or hurt when people get in my way—like won't let me take pictures or touch stuff

_____ using my creativity instead of my money (or my mom and dad's money!)

_____ not expecting everybody else to get as excited about this new hobby as I am

_____ not being discouraged if somebody points out a bunch of reasons why it can't be done

_____ being respectful of your creation, your people, and the things they've made

And, Father, I want to especially thank you for this new hobby I'm about to start: _____

_____

_____

I'll see you out there!

Love,

_____

Lily Pad

If I could observe any part of creation, it would be ...

Take It Outside!

**He is your praise; he is your God,
who performed for you those great and awesome
wonders you saw with your own eyes.**

Deuteronomy 10:21

Zooey thought she was the last person on the planet who would ever take up an outdoor hobby. For openers, she was considered "the fat girl" in elementary school, and after the first time a kid told her she was a klutz, she wouldn't even try any fun activity that required getting off the couch or too far from the refrigerator. Fun? What could possibly be fun about doing something where everyone else involved was going to tease her?

Then in seventh grade, she had to take a P.E. class, which involved gym shorts and aerobics and other things she dreaded. She was even considering just sitting on the sidelines every day and taking an F in the class, when the coach began to encourage her. The coach told Zooey she wasn't clumsy, that she was good at the aerobics exercises, and that with the muscles she had in her legs, she could pretty much outrun every other girl in the class when it came to endurance.

Zooey believed her—she should have, because it was the truth!—and started to give it her all. In the process, some surprises came her way. It wasn't long before she was helping some of the other girls with the aerobics moves. The coach put her up at the front of the class to help lead. When they ran outside, the coach told her to set a medium pace and stay with it, even if other people passed her.

To keep herself from getting bored, Zooey began to look around as she jogged on the track and discovered that she liked being outside more than she'd ever realized. (She'd never spent much time *outside* because the TV and the refrigerator were on the *inside*!)

Zooey looked beyond the schoolyard at a nearby park and wondered why she'd never taken a walk there. She watched seagulls making their way to the river and remembered that there was a special path for walkers and bicyclists there that she had never explored. It had never occurred to her that there were big, thick trees growing all around the school and that those were all over town—there was even one in her backyard she hadn't climbed since she was seven.

So Zooey started to explore those things, getting her mom to come read a book on a bench while she explored the park and convincing her to stroll with her on the River Walk. She'd just gotten to the point where she'd seen just about every inch of those places when she discovered that there was an

Adventure Club at school. The sponsor explained to her that the group met weekly to plan hikes and then went out once a month. Sometimes they took a bus to the site and hiked out from there. All she would need was a good pair of tennis shoes, which she already had for P.E. class.

"But do you think I'm too fat to keep up?" Zooey asked her.

The teacher's eyebrows sprang up to her forehead. "Fat?" she said. "I see no fat on you, girl. You look perfectly healthy!"

Zooey discovered later that afternoon when she gazed at herself in the mirror that the teacher was right. She wasn't fat anymore. The truth was, she never had been. But she'd believed she was and had let that keep her from getting out and living her life abundantly. Now that she was focusing on adventure and nature, the "fat girl" she'd always thought she was had slipped away.

She never really thought about it again as she threw herself into the Adventure Club. Ashley and her group said the kids in there were geeks, but Zooey was learning that the opinions of Ashley's friends didn't necessarily reflect those of the rest of the world. There were cool kids in the club, and they were as jazzed about hiking as she was. After the first trip up to the Pocono Mountains, they couldn't hold a candle to her in the excitement department. Zooey had found a new hobby — and a whole new world.

Could it be that there is an outdoor hobby that's perfect for you — even if you've never been "the athletic type"? Let's check it out.

✓ Check Yourself Out

Put a star next to each statement that's true for you:

_____ I used to like to play outside when I was a little kid.

_____ I've seen photographs of myself when I was younger, playing outside.

_____ At some point in my life, I've enjoyed the experience of lying in bed early in the morning, listening to the outside sounds.

_____ When I look at a picture of mountains, I think about being in them.

_____ I had a bike that I rode when I was a kid (or I still do).

_____ I water my mom's plants more than she does (or I often remind her, or at least I notice that plants need water!).

_____ I used to like to dig in the dirt when I was a kid.

_____ When I pass a field with a horse in it, I wonder what it would be like to ride one (or remember what it was like to ride one at some time).

_____ Pony rides were a big deal to me when I was a little kid.

_____ I like old-fashioned pictures of kids fishing with cane poles and a piece of string, sometimes with a dog sitting nearby.

_____ I've seen people clam digging or crabbing at the beach, and it looked like they were having fun.

_____ I might like to fish if it weren't for the worms.

_____ I'm not too afraid of the water to try going out in a canoe.

_____ At least one time when I was a kid, I camped out in my own or someone else's backyard, and it was pretty fun.

_____ I like the sound of the word "adventure" even though I don't think I've ever had one.

_____ I used to like to swim when I was a kid, even if it wasn't really swimming but just playing in the water.

_____ Those pictures of girls in old-fashioned dresses chasing butterflies with a net look really cool to me.

_____ I've seen people on roller blades and *not* thought—"Man, that looks scary."

Count up your stars and read below what your number may mean. (Remember that this is just to guide you in making a choice you might not have thought of. Your choice says nothing about you being good or bad at outdoor activities!)

If you had 13 or more stars, that probably means that you could find an outdoor hobby that you would enjoy *and* that you could do a lot of good things for yourself if you did find one and pursue it. You may have forgotten how much fun things like swimming or camping can be, and it would be neat to recapture that—on your now more-grown-up level. Or the way you think of yourself might be different now. Maybe you don't think you can do those things any-more, because now you think you have to be good at them instead of just playing. Or you might have given up those activities because they aren't considered cool by kids your age. Changing those ways of thinking can do nothing but help you, and this is one time when the changing process can be fun (no pain involved!). Read on. Try the "Just Do It" exercise for a while. See if you start finding some joy. If not, you've lost nothing.

If you had fewer than 12 stars, it *could* be that going after an outdoor hobby right now might not be your best choice. Maybe that's never been your thing. Or maybe you already do outdoorsy things for fun and are ready to expand into other areas—though no one has to try them all! That's perfectly okay. Don't force yourself to do anything that's supposed to be fun, unless you never get out from in front of the television, and in that case, a little self-persuading is in order! *But,* if you had fewer than 12 stars and you still think some of these outdoor hobbies sound fun and you aren't already involved in any, by all means, go for it! Read on! As a matter of fact, read on anyway. You never know what you might learn.

Just Do It!

We've tried to give suggestions here that won't cost you money. Anything that does call for some cash is in *italics* and is optional, which means you don't have to have it. The do-it-yourself freebie suggestions are given first each time and are usually more fun anyway.

- Before you start your outdoor hobby, make sure that you have your parents' permission and are ready to observe any limits they set, such as "No roller-blading by yourself" or "No begging for a new bike—we can't afford one right now." A number of outdoor hobbies have some real safety issues that go with them, and your parents are the best people to look into those. It's in their contract! If they decide they'd rather you didn't take up roller-blading after all, you'll have to let it go. But not to worry—there are plenty of other hobbies that are just as much fun.

- Before you commit to purchasing equipment or materials, try out the hobby first. For instance, if you think you want to have a vegetable garden of your own in the yard this spring, spend a day or an afternoon working with your mom in hers to see if spending hours in the sun, up to your elbows in dirt and fertilizer, really does light up your life. If you think camping might be the coolest thing in life, accept your friend's invitation to go camping with her and her family and try it out. A small taste is all you need to tell you whether you want the whole meal!

- Once you've decided that you'd like to do this outdoor thing on a regular basis, the first thing you need to do is get the basic equipment that's involved before you make any plans. Look for books in the library on the hobby you want to go for, or talk to an adult who has also chosen that particular hobby. Find out the least you'll need in order to be safe and have fun.

- The list may seem long, and you may see dollar signs in your head as you sigh and give up on the idea all together. But don't abandon it just because there's not enough money for you to go to the local sporting goods store and get all new stuff.

1. Look in your own garage, attic, basement, or storage shed. Maybe your parents used to camp before they had kids. Perhaps your dad doesn't have time to go fishing anymore. Your mom might have bought new gardening tools and never tossed out her old ones. Just ask permission before you claim them for your own.

2. Put up an ad on the church bulletin board saying you're looking for a used bike or a small tent or whatever. Indicate what you're ready to trade—a smaller bike, some weed pulling, that kind of thing.

3. Save up your allowance and *visit yard sales*. Take a parent with you who can test used equipment for safety and condition. That can prevent you from having a flat tire on your first bike ride or getting rained on in a leaky tent during that backyard campout.

4. Think about what you already have that might work. Maybe it *is* the same bike you've had for three years, but a seat adjustment and a little paint might make it last another six months. Perhaps you'd rather not backyard camp in your Barbie sleeping bag, but it's going to be dark—so who cares!

5. If your parents give you a "stick with this for two months and we'll talk about buying equipment" message, do what you can with what you can dig up now, and spend some time planning for what you'd like to have three months from now. Get some catalogs and a yellow highlighter and dream to your heart's content.

Unlike collecting and observing hobbies, an outdoor hobby doesn't scream for some kind of record keeping. But keeping track of your adventures in some fun way will enrich your hobby, and you'll be able to share it with people who want to hear about what you're doing. If you do decide to keep a record, you can use supplies around the house to do any of these things:

1. Come up with a log so you can write things in quickly and easily (if quick and easy are your kind of thing). If fishing is your hobby, for example, you could design a log page with columns labeled like this:

Date   Time   Type of Fish Caught   Weight   Comments

In the comments column, you could write a few notes about how it felt to haul in that giant—well, really big—bass.

2. Keep a special journal for describing your adventures. Just don't wait too long after you come home to use it, or you'll forget the really neat little details. Remember that a journal doesn't have to be perfect. In fact, you don't even have to spell everything right! It's your private record of what's important to you to remember. In the case of a fishing hobby, instead of keeping the log above, you might want to write about the way the sun came up as you made your first catch of the day.

3. Make a scrapbook so you can include pictures, artwork, or anything you want. Even if and when you move on to another hobby, you'll still have a pictorial record to go back to and be able to enjoy the experiences all over again.

• The next step is to pursue your hobby, officially, for the first time. Ways and places to do that are explained in the "Girlz Want to Know" section. Before you start out, make sure you know the rules of the road for your hobby. If you're going to a park or an outdoor pool—any public place—make it your business to read the rules for that place before you dive into the deep end or take off down the pathways on your roller-blades. "I didn't know" doesn't usually help you feel better when you get hurt.

GIRLZ want to know

✿ *SUZY: Now that I know more about outdoor hobbies, I think I'd like to ride my bike more just for fun. But I know what I'm like. I'm afraid I'll turn it into a way to build up for soccer or start trying to make my time better than the last ride every time I go out on my bicycle. How can I keep from doing that?*

It's pretty impressive that you can see that about yourself. That's half your solution right there! So for starters, check yourself every once in a while, like maybe once during a ride, to make sure those thoughts aren't crowding out the sheer enjoyment and freedom of riding.

If you find yourself racing against yesterday's time, laugh it off—right out loud. Then *do* something to keep your mind from going back there. Stop for a snack. Sing your special bike-riding song. Plan in your mind how you could decorate your bike for your next ride. Pretty soon, it will become natural for  you to have fun, and you won't even consider checking your stopwatch. Just to be on the safe side, don't even bring things like stopwatches along, and don't set up a logbook, whatever you do! Just throw your head back and love the ride (uh, but keep your eye out for cars!).

✿ *RENI: This might sound weird, but I think I'd like to go fishing. I even found some dusty old fishing rods and reels in the basement. The thing is, though—how am I going to get to a fishing spot? Come to think of it, I don't even know what a good fishing spot looks like!*

Did you say you found some fishing equipment in your basement? Doesn't that mean somebody in your house must have fished at one time? Or maybe even *both* your mom and dad? Why not ask them? See if one or both of them would like to take you. If they don't seem too eager to do that, ask them about some of their favorite fishing memories. Ask them about a nearby place where they would go fishing if they did go. "What makes a good fishing spot?" you might ask. You might even rekindle their interest.

If not, you might have to turn elsewhere—with their permission. Scope out your church and see who the fishing families are. Ask them where they fish. Tell them you'd love a lesson sometime—if your parents think that's appropriate for you to say. Most of the time, if you put a good idea out there, somebody's going to smell it and help you with it.

✿ *LILY: When I was studying some of my historical stuff, I found out girls in the Victorian era used to go butterfly hunting. I would love to do that! My dad even found a net for me in the prop room at the college theater that they said I could have. I've tried it a couple of times, and it was fun. But it would be more fun if I had some other people to do it with. The Girlz are used to my far-out ideas—and most of the time they even go along—but they just wouldn't go for this one. How do you find hobby partners?*

You put out a call for fellow butterfly hunters, of course! If that sounds like a fail-safe way for people to look at you like you have two heads, then take a creative approach. Turn a butterfly hunt into a party. Look around for other girls who seem to be reading the same kinds of books you do—the other *Anne of Green Gables* fans, the other girls who also have read their first Jane Austen novel. Look for girls who do the occasional braided thing with their hair, risk showing up in a ruffled blouse, or seem really into the poetry unit in English class.

Make Victorian-looking invitations, asking them to join you on a Saturday afternoon for lemonade, cookies, and a Victorian sport. (Be sure you plan this during butterfly season, of course!) Ask that resourceful dad of yours to help you figure out how to make nets for the other girls. You might be talking a piece of dowel, a wire coat hanger, and some netting for each one. Ask the girls to wear their almost-Green Gables best, pour the lemonade, and wait for the fun to begin!

The point is that if you're looking for new people to join in the fun of a hobby with you, it makes sense to scope out the folks who have interests similar to yours. Then make the opportunity impossible to resist.

Talking to God About It

Dear _____, (your favorite way of addressing our Father)

Do you really think I could have an outdoor hobby without my family being involved too? I mean, is that really possible? I've put stars by the things I'm most worried about:

_____ my parents saying it's okay

_____ getting the equipment I'll need

_____ finding places to do it

_____ getting people to do it with me

But there's a little spark in me that says to go for it. Will you help me know if it's a good thing to try? Will you help me with those areas? Will you especially help me with _____.

I really want to feel your pleasure and joy in everything I do. The thing that draws me to this hobby, the way I think I can glorify you in it, is _____ _____.

If I just left that blank, God, please help me as I set out in joy to find the words to fill it in!

Thanks for making life so much fun! As always and forever, I love you.

Love,

_____

Lily Pad

The perfect outdoor day looks like ...

Sports Hobbies That Don't Really Seem Like Sports

The Spirit gives life; the flesh counts for nothing. The words I have spoken to you are spirit and they are life.

John 6:63

Suzy is the athlete among the Girlz—running off to soccer practice several times a week and competing in gymnastics tournaments every couple of months. If it involves being fast or strong or coordinated, Suzy can do it, and do it better than anybody in her class. For such a soft-spoken, often timid girl, she's almost ferocious when it comes to competing in sports.

That's why it surprised some people when Suzy asked her dad to clear a space for the old Ping-Pong table in the garage, dug in the boxes for some paddles and balls, and got anybody who came along to play with her—for fun. What has really popped everybody's eyes out are Suzy's Ping-Pong rules:

- no keeping score
- no playing cutthroat
- no win-lose words

She even posted them above the table! At the first sign of anything serious during a game, that's it—she puts down her paddle and says, "I need a break. You want some juice?"

So what's up with Suzy?

It started one day at soccer practice. It wasn't even a game—it was just a scrimmage, where the team members play each other. Suzy's side wasn't doing very well. One girl in particular was really off and missed a couple of easy passes. Suzy couldn't stand it. Every time the girl made a mistake, Suzy felt her face going a deeper shade of red. She was gritting her teeth to bite back the things she wanted to yell at her teammate, but finally she couldn't hold it in any longer. Suzy kicked the ball up into the empty bleachers, stomped over to the girl, and screamed, "What's the matter with you? Do you *want* us to lose?"

There was a slight pause in the scrimmage while the coach banished Suzy to the bench. She sat miserably watching her friends play, chewing her lip, and wondering what had come over her. *Am I really a bad person?* she thought. *Do I just pretend to be nice the rest of the time—and then the real me comes out on the field?*

After practice, Suzy's coach reassured her. He said Suzy was suffering from an overdose of competition. His prescription: find a sport that she could play *with* other people in which she wouldn't play to win. She would play only for fun.

She couldn't even imagine such a thing—but since she wasn't allowed back on the soccer field until she found one, Suzy got to work right away. That night she asked her dad what kind of sport you could play without competition. He looked at her like she was nuts, her dad being a very competitive man in every area of his life. (He even raced himself every morning to see how fast he could get ready for work!)

But a little while later, he came in with a photo of him and Suzy's oldest sister when she was about six, playing Ping-Pong. He admitted that since she was practically still a baby at that time, he couldn't challenge her to a win and enjoyed batting the ball around with her.

He told Suzy that the old table was folded up against a wall in the garage and that there were balls and paddles in a box somewhere. When Suzy got excited and asked him to get the table out, he said he would, but he warned her that it was going to be almost impossible for her not to eventually turn the whole thing into a neighborhood tournament because she was loaded with competitive genes. The only way, he said jokingly, would be if she made it a rule that nobody could win and nobody could keep score.

Suzy didn't think it was funny—she thought it was a great idea—and that's what she did. At first she had to go out and recruit younger kids on her street to play with her because her friends had seen her temper before and wouldn't even touch Ping-Pong. But once the Girlz saw her in action a few times and realized she stuck to her rules, they joined in and had a blast.

So what's the fun in it for Suzy if she can't play to win?

• She can laugh and joke around while she's playing because it doesn't matter whether she's better than her fellow player or not.

- She gets to play around with fun techniques like hitting the ball from behind her back without worrying whether she'll score a point.
- She gets a big charge out of keeping a volley going for as long as she and the other player can. It's more fun than trying to make the other person miss.

Make no mistake—Suzy is still a competitive soccer player. But soccer is more fun for her now. She can let herself make a mistake at practice, and more importantly, she can let her fellow players make them! She sees that sports are *supposed* to be fun and that when competition gets *too* serious and you go after your teammates with your teeth bared, most of the fun goes out. Her Ping-Pong hobby has helped Suzy find a good balance with those competitive genes.

You might not be a competition freak like Suzy who needs toning down. In fact, you might be a person who runs the other way every time somebody suggests a game of checkers because you hate competition. If it's hard for you to enjoy sports for any reason, you might want to take up a sports hobby—one that doesn't seem like a sport at all. That may sound a little crazy, but let's take a closer look at you and see what you think then.

✓ Check Yourself Out

Circle all the words or phrases below that you think describe you now or at some time in your life:

klutz
clumsy
uncoordinated
lazy
loser
last to be picked for the team
unathletic ditz
athletically challenged
sports zero
total nerd

How many did you circle? _____

Let's see what that may tell you.

If you circled 8 or more, you probably don't think you're much of an athlete. It's okay to know that you're never going to compete in the Olympics or coach college women's basketball. What isn't so okay is thinking of yourself as somehow "less than" because you aren't Olympic material. You have other talents—everybody does—and it does *not* matter that you don't excel at sports.

But everyone can enjoy getting her body moving, have fun playing a game, and feel like part of a team without being able to hit a softball with a bat or knock herself out trying to win. Under the "Just Do It" section, you can learn to do that and at the same time banish those negative—and totally untrue—words from your thoughts.

If you circled 7 or fewer, underline the words or phrases below that describe the way you think about yourself sometimes:

> competitive
> sore loser
> impatient with poor players
> plays to win
> not always a good sport
> it doesn't matter how you play the game as long as you win

If you underlined 4 or more of those, there's a good chance you're over-competing. Don't give up the sports you're already playing, but try, like Suzy did, to find a non-sports sport that will help you remember how much fun sports are supposed to be.

In either case (or even if you fall someplace in between), try the "Just Do It" section and see where it leads you. A sport that doesn't even seem like a sport may find you on the way.

Just Do It

Read the descriptions below and see if any of them work for you or give you an idea for one that might. Put a star next to each one that sounds fun to you.

In the Games Department: These are sports that involve your mind more than your body, if that appeals to you. They do involve winning and losing, but if you play them just for the enjoyment of figuring out new moves and improving your skill (and your mind), it won't be about beating your opponent. Below are a few. It would also be fun to wander through the games section of your local toy store and see what you find. Even games like Clue and Parcheesi can work, or you can just make a hobby from board games in general, collecting used ones at yard sales and holding your own game nights.

_____ chess

_____ checkers

_____ backgammon

_____ cribbage

Just-For-Fun-Sports: These are sports, but you won't see them on ESPN—except maybe at 2:00 in the morning! Yes, they can be played with a score and a winner and loser and a competitive edge. But they don't have to be, and to benefit you as a hobby, they shouldn't be. They involve a couple of friends getting together and improving their skills while they laugh their heads off. If you never get any better at the sport, it will get boring, but becoming  more skilled at it doesn't mean you have to beat everybody on the block. Here are a few suggestions. For more, it would be fun to wander around in a sporting goods store and keep your eyes open for anything that's just for fun!

_____ Ping-Pong

_____ badminton

_____ croquet

_____ Frisbee

Unorganized Organized Sports: These are the sports you may think of as being competitive because there are organized teams around and kids seem to be playing them for trophies. But they *can* be played for the "up" feeling you get when you're just having a blast. Once again, you'll want to improve your skills just to keep it interesting, but that can happen naturally, without having to work at it to make the team or score the winning point. These are some examples. To expand the list, you can go through the sports section of the newspaper or read the week's schedule for the sports channel. Any sport that can be played professionally or for competition can also be played for fun. That's probably how it got invented in the first place!

_____ sandlot softball

_____ friendly soccer

_____ one-on-one basketball with a lowered hoop

_____ volleyball in a backyard pool — shallow end

Invent Your Own Sport: Here's where you can let your imagination run wild. Maybe it will happen after you've played a just-for-fun sport long enough that it's getting to be same old thing. You really like playing it, though, so you let your mind wander into possibilities for making it more interesting—more challenging—or more wacky! It might be fun to have a brainstorming session with your friends. You can make a list of every sport of every kind that you can think of. Then, as a group, play around with them. Can you combine some? Add a twist to one? Give it a theme? Here are some examples. Or you could even make designing wacky sports your hobby!

_____ Frisbee golf

_____ Alice in Wonderland croquet

_____ tricycle racing

_____ silly swimming (where you make up new strokes with fun names)

Unique and even silly sports can give you confidence about your ability to play and enjoy playing without having to be good enough. Chances are, though, they aren't going to become lifelong hobbies. So it's more important than ever for you not to spend money or ask your parents to spend money on equipment. Look back at the chapter on outdoor hobbies for suggestions on how to be creative when it comes to balls and bats and racquets and things. Be sure to read the part about safety—even non-sports sports have their danger spots.

GIRLZ want to know

❀ *RENI: I'm not as competitive as Suzy, but I do like things to be right, you know? I'm afraid if I tried one of these non-sports sports, I would have trouble keeping it fun. I can just see me now, looking for somebody to give me lessons in backyard bowling!*

It would be easy to *say*, "Oh, just go out there and have fun!"—but it might not be so easy for you to *do*. Maybe these suggestions will help.

- Come up with some rules like Suzy's. You can even use hers if you want. Keep them posted near the playing area. Reward yourself for following them—but only if you think about it. Don't keep a record of how many games you play without breaking one of your own rules!

- Stop playing if you find yourself getting frustrated or not having any fun. You might need to take a break, or you may need to ask yourself what's going on with you. If you keep playing, you'll develop bad feelings about the whole thing, and it won't provide you with the joy that a hobby should. Organized sports are sometimes frustrating and un-fun, and the players learn from that experience, but this is a hobby, not a championship team. If it isn't fun, don't do it.

- If somebody else tries to make your game serious, that's a good time to break for Gatorade! Don't let anybody ruin the fun.

❀ *LILY: The only thing with this kind of hobby is that it doesn't seem to have a way of keeping a record like the other ones do, and that's half the fun for me. Is it okay to write stuff down about it, or is that wrong?*

The best thing about hobbies is that, except for the safety factor, there really is no wrong. Sure you can write things down. In fact, it might even be fun to chronicle the season. You could keep a scrapbook, or better yet, a bulletin board in the playing area where you keep Polaroid pictures with funny captions. Or

Reni lines up her shot!

Zooey gets stuck!

what about a big sheet of white paper on the wall—the kind
that comes on a roll, perhaps—where everyone
who plays can write comments? Remember, no
recording scores or wins and losses because there
are none!

❧ *ZOOEY: I've always gotten teased a lot, so I try to avoid it
whenever I can. How can I get people to play with me without being told—again—that I'm a complete geek? And please don't tell
me just not to worry about what other people think. I've tried that,
and it didn't work.*

That's so hard, especially at this time in your life. Anyone who tells
you not to worry about what other people think is giving you good
advice, but advice that's almost impossible to follow. It *is* a bummer to
be called a geek or be given those eye-rolling looks. It *is* tough not to
be hurt by other people's bad behavior. So what we've said many times
before needs repeating: since you can't control those people who insist
on being hateful, don't put yourself into a situation where they can
hurt you. You know who they are—whether it's kids at school or your
brother or even one of your friends. Don't invite them to play with you.
Don't even tell them what you do in your spare time.

That leaves us with the question of where to find people who might get
a kick out of making up Frisbee games with you (or whatever non-sport
you've decided to try). Why not invite as many people as you know who
are not likely to tease you to come over one Saturday afternoon? Ask them
to bring Frisbees or whatever equipment it is you need. Make that the
focus of a backyard bash with sandwiches and chips—if that's okay with
your mom. You'll have better luck with her if you make all the sandwiches, sweep the patio, etc. As the Frisbee is tossed around, you'll see
who gets a kick out of it and who gets bored and heads for the snack
table. Later you can tell the Frisbee lovers your idea, which they'll
probably love. Can you see how this will probably work for just about
any funky sport you choose?

Talking To God About It

Dear _____, *(your favorite way of addressing our Father)*

You know something—you're really a fun God! I know you have to watch out for us and correct us and all, but you have fun too. If that weren't true, we wouldn't know how to create all this neat stuff, seeing how we're created in your image. When I think of you being fun, I think of _____.

I know this hobby is for my benefit as well as for my enjoyment, so would you help me, God, with the things I've put crosses by below?

_____ *letting loose of being so competitive about everything*

_____ *keeping myself from ruining the real sports I play by being too anxious to win*

_____ *being able to enjoy myself instead of expecting myself to be perfect (or everybody around me!)*

_____ *getting some confidence in my body and the way I move*

_____ *not thinking of myself as a klutz or a loser*

And, God, will you help me round up fellow players? I'd especially like to play with _____.

I know one thing for sure, you'll be right there playing beside me, and it'll be a God thing!

Love,

_____

Lily Pad

My favorite sport is ...

It's a Little Unusual, But It's My Hobby

**For you created my inmost being;
you knit me together in my mother's womb.**
Psalm 139:13

Leave it to **Lily** to come up with a hobby that boggles the mind! If you'll recall from chapter 1, she's becoming an expert on the medieval period—reading everything she can get her hands on, building a model of a medieval castle, designing her own medieval costumes. She's just the kind of person, as you know by now, who never does anything halfway and is never content with choosing from a list.

Her brothers call her "weird" and "strange" and "wacko." Some kids at school—like Ashley and that crowd—translate that into "nerd," "geek," and "so OUT there."

But in reality—God's reality—Lily is "unique," "distinctive," "special," and "one of a kind." And so are you!

God created each one of us to be absolutely different from everybody else. Even identical twins don't look *exactly* alike when you get down to moles and birthmarks, and they sure don't think, act, and react precisely the same way, either. Each of us is a unique, distinctive, special, one-of-a-kind individual, so why shouldn't our hobbies reflect that?

There's nothing wrong with having the same hobby that dozens of other people have, as long as it's the hobby you really want and as long as you aren't involved in it just because everybody else is. But it's also okay—and more than okay!—to explore ideas for a hobby that you can shape into something that is totally *you*. This chapter—and the Girlz!—can help you do that.

✓ Check Yourself Out

Even if you're convinced that you are not creative enough to come up with your own hobby (in which case, please read *The Creativity Book* to get straight on that!), go ahead and take this quiz. You may be surprised to find ideas popping into your head or excitement throbbing through those veins of yours. Or you may think, "Yeah, this sounds good, but I'm fine with the hobby I have." But some of the things you discover here might help you jazz up your rock collection or your badminton bashes. Besides, you have absolutely nothing to lose by exploring options, right?

Part 1

Put a star beside each item in this list that sounds interesting to you. Try to choose at least one that catches your eye, even if it isn't *totally* fascinating to you.

_____ traveling to a foreign country

_____ meeting a famous author

_____ going back in time

_____ designing something—anything

_____ taking lessons from a famous artist

_____ being coached by a pro coach

_____ seeing an awesome collection up close and personal

_____ working in a lab with real researchers

_____ seeing every game a pro team plays in a season

_____ raising purebred animals (dogs, cats, horses, birds, wild animals)

Let's see what that might mean.

If you starred 7 or more, the whole *idea* of an unusual, design-it-yourself hobby probably really appeals to you—and there are several avenues you could take and have a ball. Definitely read on!

If you starred fewer than 7, you might need a little more inspiration to get you excited about an unusual, design-it-yourself hobby. Maybe it isn't your thing—or maybe you need more information. Continue on, just to see what the possibilities might be.

Part 2

In these pairs of assignments, choose the *one* in each pair that you would rather do. (Wouldn't it be nice if you really had these kinds of choices in school?)

Column A	Column B
_____ Do an exercise on commas.	_____ Write a paragraph about the subject of your choice to show that you understand how to use commas.
_____ Read a history chapter and answer the questions.	_____ Read a history chapter and pretend you are one of the historical figures telling what happened, wearing a costume you put together.
_____ Watch the teacher do a science experiment and take a quiz on it.	_____ Study a science topic and make up an experiment to show you understand it.
_____ Read a book and fill out a form for a book report.	_____ Read a book and build a model of the setting; use small figures of the characters to re-enact the plot.
_____ Match the names of some painters to their paintings.	_____ Look at all the paintings by a painter you like and learn about the painter's life and why he or she painted the way he or she did, then create a mini-gallery of the painter's work.

If more of your checks were in Column B than in Column A, chances are you'd enjoy an unusual hobby that means doing research and then doing something hands-on with what you find out. That's especially true if you starred several of the activities in PART 1. Read on—some hobby adventures could be waiting for you!

If more of your checks were in Column A than in Column B, you may be a person who would much rather show what you know in a straightforward, let's-get-it-done way so you can move on to the next thing—which is perfectly fine. You probably have other things to do, and *those* things will lead you to your hobby. But read on anyway. You may surprise yourself.

Just Do It

So let's say this whole idea of creating your own like-no-other hobby really appeals to you. Or let's admit you're still not sure and you're just reading on to give it a shot. In either case, how would you put your hobby together?

Let's go through a step-by-step approach and see where it takes you. Even if you *know* you'll never pursue the hobby you come up with, the process alone can be fun.

Step 1: Look back at the items you put stars by in PART 1 of the "Check Yourself Out" quiz. Pick the one that sounds like the most fun and write it here: _____

Step 2: Circle the topic group below that seems to best fit what you've written on the line. (There is no right or wrong—it's your call.)

1. Travel/foreign countries/geography
2. History/historical customs/particular periods of history
3. Art/artists/how to paint, draw, or sculpt
4. Museums/famous collections
5. Sports/coaching/sports fans
6. Books/writers/literature
7. Design/fashion/architecture/inventions
8. Science/biology/chemistry/medicine/scientific research
9. Animals/veterinarians/breeding

Step 3: Think about exactly what interests you the most about that topic group. Brainstorm in this space. (Brainstorming means write down all the cool things that come into your head. Don't worry about complete sentences or spelling—yea!)

Example: Travel/foreign countries/geography/Switzerland/trains/native costumes

_____
_____
_____
_____

HINT: If this seems hard, maybe looking at a general book from the library or a magazine on your topic will help you get ideas.

Step 4: Now use your imagination to see if you can put together the very things that fascinate you most. Some examples might help.

LILY

Step 1: Traveling to a foreign country

Step 2: History/historical customs/particular periods of history

Step 3: The medieval period fashions: how they lived, like the castles and stuff

Step 4: I could study about the medieval period, read everything! Look at pictures of castles and read how they were built and stuff. I could collect pictures of medieval costumes—and design my own—maybe even make some for dolls. If that doesn't work, I could make paper dolls, design their costumes on paper, cut them out, and dress them up. Oh—I could also build a model of a medieval castle and put the dolls in their costumes in it.

RENI

Step 1: Meeting a famous author

Step 2: Books/writers/literature

Step 3: Since I already collect old kids' series books— Nancy Drew/cool covers/the author, Carolyn Keene/how the Nancy Drew books have changed over the years

Step 4: I could use the Nancy Drew series I've already collected and find out everything I can about it instead of just *having* it. I could look up the author. I could try to find all the titles in the three different times it was published and see how they're different. Some of the ones I've collected don't have those paper jacket covers, so I could design my own covers and write on the back stuff I've learned about the series and the author. Maybe I could start a Nancy Drew journal and write like I was her on each day of one of her adventures—that would be so cool!

SUZY

Step 1: Being coached by a pro coach

Step 2: Sports/coaching/sports fans

Step 3: Gymnasts in the Olympics/especially old ones like Mary Lou Retton and Nadia Comenici/what it must be like to work with a professional coach

Step 4: I could check out those videos from the library—"Highlights of the Summer Olympics, 1984" and watch Mary Lou and Nadia. I could also read old articles in the library files and check out books, especially about their coaches. Then I could put together a scrapbook, maybe even write my own articles. I could even pretend I was there.

As you pull your hobby together, it might help you to have some suggested activities. Circle any of the ones below that sound fun to you and see if you can use them in your hobby.

read	look at pictures
see movies	see plays
make a scrapbook	make a photo album
draw	build a model
use the library	interview experts
make a map	create displays
go to museums	go on a tour
re-enact an event	

Your STEP 4 Plan: The best part is that once you have a plan, you can change it as you go along and discover better, more fun ways to do things. After all, it's *your* hobby, so there is no right or wrong!

GIRLZ want to know

🏵 *ZOOEY: My mom doesn't like me to get carried away with stuff. She always tells me to keep things simple. I would love to have a hobby of pretending I'm about to travel to different places and plan my trips, but I can just hear my mom say I can't clutter up my room with brochures or tack maps on my walls. I guess I should just forget that hobby.*

It's in a mother's contract to keep clutter from taking over the house, so your mom's just doing her thing. But you can still have your hobby and play by the rules at the same time. Try following these guidelines.

- Keep everything organized so that the word "clutter" never enters your mom's mind when she walks into your room. Keep folders or a scrapbook for your brochures and maps. Line your travel books up neatly on your bookshelf or keep them in a tidy stack beside the bed. Besides, when you can put your hands on what you want when you want it, you'll enjoy your hobby more.

- Confine your hobby to one corner of your room. Maybe your chair could become your "Armchair Travel" chair and you could keep your books stacked beside it and your scrapbook or file folders pushed under it, rather than turning your entire bedroom into a travel agency.

- You can even arrange all your hobby stuff so that you can fold it up and put it away and get it back out easily. Maybe it all goes in one old duffle bag no one's using anymore. Or maybe you have a small bulletin board for your current "trip plan" that you can stick in the back of your closet when you aren't focusing on your hobby. Just be sure to put it all away when you're finished with a hobby session.

- See if you can compromise with your mom. First of all, it sounds like you're giving up on the idea before you even talk to her. Why not approach her with your plan for organizing and storing your stuff, so she'll see that you're already thinking about the clutter factor? (She'll probably be impressed!) Suggest that corner of your room and ask if you can have just one map on the wall there. Offer to use that sticky poster gum instead of putting holes in your wallpaper with tacks. Be open to her suggestions, and if she says no to anything, accept it as final. That's also in a mother's contract!

❧ *KRESHA: I think I would like to make a gallery of paintings of people. I already know that I can use the walls of my closet to put up paintings I will copy from art books in the school library. But I'm afraid I will get half-way finished and then quit. I do that — I get bored with things very fast.*

Lots of times when people get bored quickly, it's because they aren't challenged enough. What they're doing is way too easy, and once they get it down pat, they lose interest. (There are other reasons for quick boredom, but this one is more than likely true for you.) Here are some things for you to think about.

- Go ahead and start. Whatever you do is going to be fun for you as long as it lasts, so what have you got to lose?

- If it gets boring, don't quit right away. See if you can't jazz it up a little to keep your interest alive. Try specializing in *one* artist's paintings of people and challenge yourself to find pictures of all of them. Add your own original paintings to the gallery. Have a gallery opening for your friends. Transfer the exhibit to the garage, the backyard, or the family room for an afternoon (with your mom's permission) and serve a snack for friends to munch on while you give them the gallery tour. (Just be

sure to invite only people who will appreciate it. This might not be the time to play hostess to Shad Shifferdecker.)

- Knowing that you tend to abandon projects halfway through, don't invest too much money into your hobby or ask your mom to buy you big items like easels and professional paint sets. If you *do* stick with it, then you can start saving for those kinds of things. If you move on to another hobby within a few weeks, there will be no guilt about all the funds that went into it.

- It's okay if you don't stick with a hobby for the rest of your life—or the rest of the school year—or the rest of the week. If jazzing it up doesn't add a new spark to your hobby, then go ahead and move on. As long as you enjoyed it while you were doing it, that's what counts. If someone tells you that you're a person who never finishes anything, never follows through, remind yourself that, for Pete's sake, you're 10 (or 8 or even 12). This is a time for exploring what interests you—not for pinning yourself down to a lifelong hobby.

✿ *SUZY: I've come up with a plan, but I've decided not to do it. If this whole design-your-own-hobby idea isn't my thing, doesn't that mean I'm just a boring person?*

Uh, how about *no!* Everybody is different. God made us that way, and what God wants is for us to be exactly who we are. So in the first place, you aren't a boring person if you aren't gung-ho about creating a one-of-a-kind hobby. If you truly want to put your energy someplace else, then you are being true to the person God made you to be. In the second place, as long as you have a hobby you love, one that relaxes and refreshes you and brings you healthy pleasure, don't worry about what it is. Just make sure it's *you.* (And wouldn't it be dull if all of us were exactly alike?)

Talking to God About It

Dear _____, *(your favorite way of addressing God)*

I want to be exactly who you want me to be, right down to what I choose as a hobby. This unusual hobby thing is one more way I could do that. How I feel about it right now is:

_____ *I'm totally excited about it and can't wait to get started.*

_____ *I'm surprised something like this even exists and I'm thinking about it.*

_____ *I'm not sure this is for me.*

_____ *I don't want to do this.*

That's how I feel. Will you please show me what you want me to do with that? After all, I want my choices to be lined up with yours. I'm especially concerned about _____.

Most of all, God, I want to be the best me I can be, since you made me. I pray that you will help me to allow my hobby—whatever it is—to help move me in a fun way in that direction. Please help me, right now, to stop and close my eyes and listen for you in silence and peace. In fact, please help me to do that every time I'm playing with my hobby. Let me feel your pleasure.

I love you—

_____

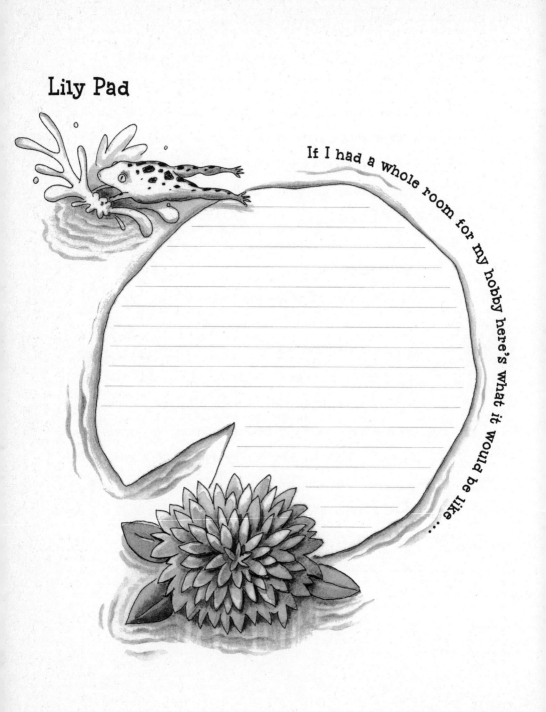

Lily Pad

If I had a whole room for my hobby here's what it would be like ...

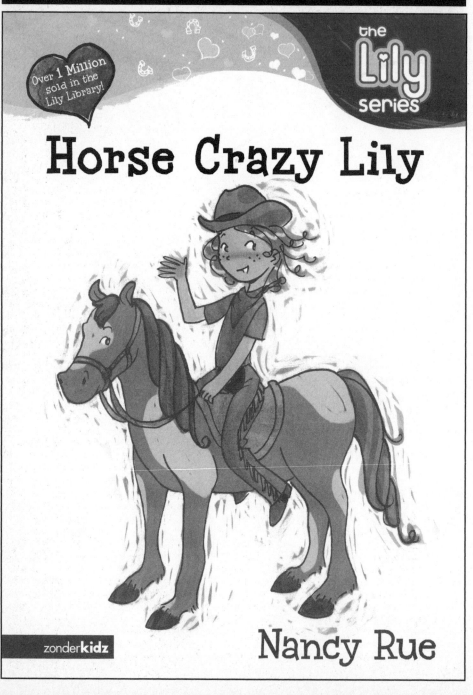

Horse Crazy Lily

Nancy Rue

Chapter 1

Hey, Lily—you comin' or what?"

Lily Robbins glared into the mirror she was standing in front of. She was looking at her own redheaded self, but the glare was intended for her seventeen-year-old brother, Art. He was two floors down and probably tossing his keys from one hand to the other.

"Like he has so much to do on a Saturday afternoon," Lily said to the mirror.

But he *had* agreed to drive her out to Suzy's birthday party.

With a sigh, she untangled her way-long-for-a-twelve-year-old legs and got to the door, where she poked her curly head out and yelled back, "Don't have a cow! I'll be right down."

"Define 'right down,'" Art yelled back.

"Two minutes."

"I'm pulling out of the driveway in exactly two minutes."

Lily scrambled to the closet and dragged out the boots she'd cleaned up for Suzy's party. They brought on a grin. What a great idea Suzy had come up with for her birthday—an afternoon of horseback riding for her and all the Girlz—Lily, Zooey, Reni, and

Kresha. Lily had never been on a horse, though she'd always thought it sounded way cool. She felt like this was as much a present for her as for Suzy.

Lily glanced at her watch and then whipped her mane of curls around, looking for the gift she'd taken a half hour to wrap. She had put it right on the bed—and it should be easy to spot.

Since she'd moved into her new room up here in the attic a week ago, she hadn't had a chance to decorate—what her mother referred to as "cluttering up the place." The only things currently cluttering it were her stuffed animals. She could barely function without them, especially the giant panda, China, who she leaned against during her talking-to-God time every night—with Otto by her side, of course.

"Otto!" Lily said.

She heard him grunt from under the bed, and she dove for it.

"Tell me you don't have Suzy's present!" she said as she lifted up the dust ruffle.

Otto, her little gray mutt, blinked at her through the darkness.

"You do—you are *so* evil!"

Lily made a snatch for the blue-covered package and managed to get hold of the ribbon. While Otto tugged one way, she yanked the other and pulled dog and gift out into daylight. Otto's scruffy top hair stood up on end.

"I'm lee-ving—" Art called from below.

"Don't! I'm coming!" Lily cried. Grabbing onto the gift—and dangling Otto in midair in the process—she grabbed her denim jacket with her free hand and tore down both flights of stairs. Otto growled and snarled the whole way, but he didn't loosen his little jaws of steel, in spite of Lily's steady stream of "Drop it, you little demon seed! I spent my whole last week's allowance on that!"

Art, arms folded, was waiting at the bottom of the stairs.

"Grab him, Art," Lily said. "Make him let go."

"You gotta be kidding," Art said. He took a step backward. "I'm not touching that dog. He'll bite my hand off."

"What in the world—" Mom said. She appeared out of the dining room, dust rag in one hand, can of furniture polish in the other. Her mouth twitched—in that way it did instead of going into a whole smile. "Otto," she said in her crisp coach's voice. "Drop it."

Otto, of course, didn't—at least not until Mom sprayed some polish into the air above her head. Otto let go of the present and, tucking his tail between his scrawny legs, disappeared up the stairs. He didn't like spray cans.

"Can we *go* now?" Art said.

"Have fun," Mom said. "And, Lil—don't make any plans to spend the night with anybody tonight. You know tomorrow is a big day."

Lily nodded as she ran toward Art's Subaru—nicknamed Ruby Sue. She managed to slide in before Art got it into gear.

"It's that place over in Columbus, right?" Art said.

"Uh-huh."

"Could she have picked a place farther away?"

"It's the only riding stables in South Jersey, I think," Lily said.

"Tha-at's an exaggeration." Art had picked up a new habit of dragging out his words in a bored voice. Lily thought it must be some cool thing musicians did.

"So—what do you think this Tessa chick is going to be like?" he said with a snicker. "Her mother must have really had it in for her to give her a name like Tessa. What's thaaat about?"

Lily rolled her eyes in his direction. "Her mother probably *did* have it in for her, or she wouldn't have been in all those foster homes.

And we're not supposed to talk about all the stuff that's happened to her unless she brings it up, remember?"

"Like I'm going to forget. We heard it about a dozen times."

Lily had to agree—he was right about that. Ever since Mom and Dad had found out that the adoption agency had a child for them, they'd been holding family meetings to talk about Tessa, who was about to become their nine-year-old sister.

"She's had a rough time," Dad had explained. "She hasn't had any of the things you kids have had, including love or security or a family."

Mom was a little more direct: "You can't be doing your brother-and-sister routine while she's getting adjusted. No teasing—no kicking under the table—am I clear?"

"Have you noticed how different they are lately when they talk about her?" Art said now. "Now that they've actually met her?"

"No," Lily said. "Well—I did notice that Mom's cleaning the entire house with a toothbrush to get ready for her. You think Tessa's a neat freak?"

Art shook his head. "I saw a list of child psychologists on Dad's desk."

"Don't they send, like, mental patients to them?"

"Nah—half the kids I know are in therapy," Art said. "Whatever the chick's got going on, it's probably not that big a deal. I think Mom and Dad are freakin' a little."

The rest of the way to the stables, Lily forgot about horses and thought about Tessa. The Robbinses had known for a while that they were going to adopt a child, and Lily had been all over it—another girl to help her survive two brothers. She'd gotten excited about fixing up her old room for Tessa, but Mom had said they should just paint it white and let her decorate it how she wanted to, since she'd never had her own room before.

When Mom and Dad had come back from meeting her, Lily had gone to Mom with a list of possible sister activities they could do together. Mom had twisted her mouth a little and then said, "I know how you are, Lil—everything 950 percent—but, hon, you can't take Tessa on as your latest thing. Don't start reading child psychology books—"

"Mom, I'm so over trying to find my thing—"

"Good—then let's just let her get settled in and get to know her."

So Lily had been forced to put the whole thing in the back of her mind, behind math homework and Shakespeare Club and, of course, Girlz Only Group. She'd prayed for Tessa every night, but that was about all. Until now.

What if she's in a gang or something? she thought. *Is she gonna get off the plane tomorrow with a tattoo?*

"So is this it?" Art said. "Double H Stables." He snickered again. "Now thaaat's original."

"Herbert Hajek, Owner," Lily read from the plank that hung under the Double H logo on the gate that Art had pulled up to. "Of *course* it's going to be Double H. What else would they call it?"

Art raised an eyebrow in the direction of the tiny stables tucked between two maple trees. "Don't get your hopes up, Lil," he said. "I don't think this guy raises thoroughbreds."

"Reni's mom's bringing me home," Lily said as she climbed out of Ruby Sue. Which was good, because she'd had about enough of Art making everything sound worse than it was.

She forgot about Art—and Tessa—the minute Zooey, Kresha, Suzy, and Reni burst out of the stables, all wearing jeans and boots and bandanas tied to various places.

"This is going to be the *best*!" Zooey said as she tugged at Lily's arm. "We each get to ride our own horse and—"

"I get the wery strong horse!" Kresha said. Lily knew she was excited because her Croatian accent was slipping in. W's replaced v's when that happened.

Reni grabbed Lily's hand—the one Zooey *wasn't* wringing out like a dishrag—and tugged her toward the stables. She didn't have to say anything. Best friends, Lily had discovered, could communicate without words. Reni's chocolate-brown eyes, dancing in the glow of her matching-brown face, said that for once Zooey wasn't exaggerating. It was going to be awesome.

Lily let them usher her into the stables. "Awesome" didn't even begin to describe what she saw when they finally let go of her and let her look around.

It was dim inside, but even in the half-light she could tell the wooden floors were swept clean. The sun that crept in from the open doors on the other end brought eight stalls into view, four on either side of the wide hallway, each with the top half of its door open.

I bet that's where you prop yourself up to give the horses apples and sugar cubes and stuff, Lily thought. The smell was a mixture of hay and leather and—okay, maybe the *faint* odor of horse poop. But nothing had ever smelled as good.

"You girlies ready to ride?" said a voice from the open doorway.

Lily could make out only a silhouette as the Girlz all ran out to him. What she found in the sunlight was a man not much taller than her own five-foot-five—tall for a seventh grader but not for a man who had shoulders that looked like a set of football pads. She decided he'd be a lot taller if he weren't quite so bow-legged.

"I'll take that as a yes," the man said as the Girlz swarmed around him. He was wearing a blue bandana, tied tightly around his head so that he slightly resembled a cue ball with bright eyes. Lily didn't have a chance to see what color they were before he planted a battered hat onto his head and pulled the brim down almost to his nose.

"This is Herbie," Zooey said, giggling like a piccolo.

Herbie nodded at Lily and then at the line of horses that waited patiently along the wide dirt path the Girlz were standing on.

"First thing, Georgie and I will get you girlies up in those saddles," he said. His voice was as clipped and snappy as any other South Jersey accent Lily had ever heard. *That's funny,* she thought. *I expected him to talk like he was from Texas or something.*

That didn't make the idea of climbing up into one of those saddles any less exciting — or any less scary.

As Herbie showed Suzy how to put one foot in the stirrup and hoist herself up so she could swing the other leg over the saddle, Reni pointed to a horse the color of a brownie with a crooked white marking on his face that was shaped just like milk pouring out of a pitcher.

"This one's Big Jake," Reni said. "He's yours." Her voice took on a hint of envy. "I think he's the biggest one of all."

Lily agreed, but she couldn't nod her head. She'd never been this close to a horse before, and she'd never known they were quite this big. She had to look up to see under his neck, which he was now tossing around like he was impatient to get this party started.

Lily stood staring at him while the rest of the Girlz swung up into their saddles. Her mouth was starting to go dry.

Maybe this wasn't such a good idea, she thought, trying to lick her lips. *This is a big animal. I don't know what to do with something like this — yikes!*

"Your turn, girlie," Herbie said. He nodded at the stirrup. "Put your left foot right in there."

Lily felt a long pang of fear go through her—but she managed to stick her right foot into the stirrup. Herbie shook his head.

"Oh, sorry!" Lily said. "I always get right and left mixed up—" Actually, she never did, but right now her thoughts were like a herd of terrified ants.

When she finally fumbled her way into the saddle, her long right leg flailing the air for one endless, embarrassing moment before her foot found the other stirrup, Herbie said, "All right, girlies. We're all going to be together so I'll be watching your horses, but there are a few things you need to know."

Yeah, Lily thought. *Like how to get down!* She leaned over to look at the ground. The height was dizzying.

What if I fall? Lily thought. *I could break a leg! Or my neck!*

"That's all you need to know, " Herbie said. He started off toward the one empty-saddled horse on the path and then stopped. "Oh, one more thing—if you have any trouble with your horse, just say—in a calm voice, now—'I have a situation.' " He tipped his head back to look up at them. "You girlies ready to ride?"

He was answered with an assortment of yeses and giggles. But Lily didn't join in. She wanted to shout right now—"I have a situation! I don't want to go!"

But Big Jake threw his head back and shook his stringy mane and blew air out of his nostrils. *He* obviously *did.*

No sooner had the line of horses begun to move—one steed's nose buried in the tail of the one in front of it—than Big Jake tossed his head once more. And then he took off—ahead of the others—with Lily hanging on.

She screamed for all she was worth, "I have a situation!"

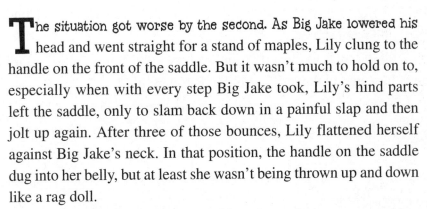

Chapter 2

The situation got worse by the second. As Big Jake lowered his head and went straight for a stand of maples, Lily clung to the handle on the front of the saddle. But it wasn't much to hold on to, especially when with every step Big Jake took, Lily's hind parts left the saddle, only to slam back down in a painful slap and then jolt up again. After three of those bounces, Lily flattened herself against Big Jake's neck. In that position, the handle on the saddle dug into her belly, but at least she wasn't being thrown up and down like a rag doll.

Lily grabbed around for something else to hang on to, and her hands found a fistful of Jake's mane on one side and a leather strap on the other. She got a death grip on both and cocked her head up so she could see where they were going.

Bad move. There was a tree limb straight ahead, ready to smack her right in the forehead. Big Jake lowered his head some more, and Lily let hers go down with him. The shadows of tree limbs dappled them from all around, so Lily didn't dare look up again. It was all she could do to hold on anyway. Sliding from side to side, she squeezed her eyes shut to try to block out the vision of herself hanging upside down underneath Big Jake as he plunged toward wherever it was he was so dead set on going.

Jake took a sudden veer off to the left, and Lily felt herself slipping, so she clamped her knees into the horse's sides to keep herself from going down. That helped her stay in place, but Big Jake seemed to like that—and ran even faster. Lily was sure if she raised up so much as an inch, she'd be beheaded.

It wasn't until Big Jake cleared the trees that Lily chanced a peek. Directly in front of them was the creek, ribboning its shiny way along at the bottom of a five-foot drop.

Lily had just opened her mouth to scream again when there was another sound—the pounding of a second set of hoof beats behind her, and then a shout.

"Pull the reins to the left, girlie!" a Jersey voice was calling. "Pull them hard and to the left—and don't stop pulling!"

Lily looked around wildly. Reins? Did she have those?

With Big Jake gaining on the creek, there was no time to get a definition. Lily just yanked what was currently in her hand to the left. Big Jake pulled his head sideways with a jerk, and Lily gave a squeal and started to let go.

"Keep pulling!" she could hear Herbie shouting beside her. "Hard to the left! Grab the other rein!"

His horse was out in front of hers now, and he seemed to be stopping.

I'll run over you! Lily wanted to scream.

But Big Jake was finally turning himself to the left—and to the left—and to the left—so that suddenly he—and Lily—were moving in a tight circle.

"That's it!" Herbie shouted. "Keep pulling to the left, hard as you can!"

It was only then that Lily realized she was the one pulling Big Jake into a circle. Above the din of Herbie's shouting and Jake's hooves clomping in the dirt, she could hear Jake protesting with a snort. But he was slowing down.

When he came to a reluctant stop, head tossing and hooves pawing, he was right in front of Herbie. And Lily was still on him.

She dropped what she now knew were the reins so she could cover her face with her hands, but Herbie snatched them up and stuck them back into her hands.

"Keep him under control, girlie," Herbie said. "Let him know who's boss."

"*He's* boss!" Lily cried.

"Don't pick your reins up," Herbie said. "Just hold them right in front of you and tell him, 'Whoa, Jake.'"

Lily felt like an idiot, but she said "Whoa, Jake." She would have said anything to avoid another flight for the creek.

Jake blew air out of his nostrils again, but he didn't move, except to stomp a little. Lily gave him another "Whoa, Jake," just to be on the safe side, and he stopped.

Herbie chuckled. "Looks to me like you're the boss now, girlie."

"I'm so sorry," Lily said. "I don't know what I did wrong—he just took off—"

Jake took a few steps forward. Lily jerked back on the reins. He settled down again.

"You can't be talking with your hands when you're holding the reins," Herbie said, grinning. "That will be the one hurdle you'll have to overcome in riding."

"If I ever get on a horse again!" Lily said.

Herbie jerked his chin up and down. "Just pick up the reins slowly," he said, "and kick your heels just gently against his sides."

"I'll hurt him!" Lily said.

"You're not going to hurt the horse. Just a little kick and pick up the reins."

"What's going to happen?" Lily said, still keeping the reins so flat against the saddle they were about to become joined.

"The horse is going to walk forward."

"Oh," Lily said. She looked at Herbie, whose bright eyes were smiling at her from under the brim of the hat that was wearing him. "You're gonna be right here?"

"Right here," he said.

Lily took a deep breath and slowly lifted the reins. "Okay, Jake," she said. "You heard that. We're going to walk — not run."

Then with another breath that she didn't let out, Lily bounced her heels against the big horse's sides. Like a miracle, he moved forward, placing his hooves politely one in front of the other and bobbing his head up and down with each step.

"Yikes!" Lily said. "I'm riding a horse!"

"You've been riding a horse ever since you got on," Herbie said, his horse rocking lazily beside hers as they moved toward the stables. "She's a natural. Isn't she, Jiminy?" He gave his horse's black mane a tousle with his fingers.

"Nuh-uh!" Lily said. "I didn't even know what a rein was!"

She cringed a little, waiting for the teacher question: Where were you when I was explaining all that? But Herbie was shaking his head.

"Most people would have fallen off," he said. "You used your natural instincts to keep yourself on." He chuckled. "Only thing was, you

were giving him the signals to go even faster. Jake's a good boy—
he'll do whatever you tell him."

"*I* was telling him to go faster?"

"The point is, you have a natural seat on a horse. A few more lessons, and you'll be on your way to becoming a fine horsewoman."

"Me?" Lily said. "But where would I get lessons?"

"I give them," Herbie said. "Hello, girlies!"

He stopped beside the line of Girlz, who were still mounted and
staring open-mouthed at Lily.

"You are okay, Lee-lee?" Kresha said.

"She's perfect, this girl," Herbie said.

Zooey's gray eyes were the size of wagon wheels. "Weren't you
scared, Lily? I'd have been so scared. I thought you were going to be
killed."

Herbie laughed his deep chuckle. "We haven't had anybody die
here yet," he said.

Suzy gave a nervous giggle. "Can we still ride?" she said.

"That's what we came out here to do, isn't it?" Herbie nodded his
head toward Suzy's horse. "Let me just get in front of you, girlie, and
we'll be on our way."

"Should Lily still be in the back?" Reni said. "What if her horse
gets away again?"

"Don't you have another horse?" Zooey said. "Maybe a slower
one?"

Herbie continued to make his way to the front of the line. When
he got there, he looked over his shoulder. "Girlies, Lily is going to be
fine," he said. Then he tipped his hat up with one finger, winked at
Lily, and turned back around.

"Head 'em up," he said. "Move 'em out!"

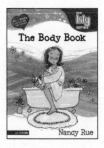

Lily and the Creep (Book Three)
Softcover • ISBN-10: 0-310-23252-X
ISBN-13: 978-0-310-23252-0
Lily learns what it means to be a child of God
and how to develop God's image in herself.

The Buddy Book
Softcover • ISBN-10: 0-310-70064-7
ISBN-13: 978-0-310-70064-7
(Companion Nonfiction to *Lily and the Creep*)
The Buddy Book is all about relationships—why they're important,
how lousy your life can be if they're crummy, what makes a good
one, and how God is the Counselor for all of them.

Lily's Ultimate Party (Book Four)
Softcover • ISBN-10: 0-310-23253-8
ISBN-13: 978-0-310-23253-7
After Lily's plans for the "ultimate" party fall apart, her grandmother shows
Lily that having a party for the right reasons will help to make it a success.

The Best Bash Book
Softcover • ISBN-10: 0-310-70065-5
ISBN-13: 978-0-310-70065-4
(Companion Nonfiction to *Lily's Ultimate Party*)
The Best Bash Book provides fun party ideas and alternatives,
as well as etiquette for hosting and attending parties.

Ask Lily (Book Five)
Softcover • ISBN-10: 0-310-23254-6
ISBN-13: 978-0-310-23254-4
Lily becomes the "Answer Girl" and gives
anonymous advice in the school newspaper.

The Blurry Rules Book
Softcover • ISBN-10: 0-310-70152-X
ISBN-13: 978-0-310-70152-1
(Companion Nonfiction to *Ask Lily*)
Explaining ethics for an 8-12 year old girl! You will discover that although there
may not always be an easy answer or a concrete rule, there's always a God answer.

Available now at your local bookstore!

Lily the Rebel (Book Six)

Softcover • ISBN-10: 0-310-23255-4
ISBN-13: 978-0-310-23255-1

Lily starts to question the rules at home and at school and decides she may not want to follow the rules.

The It's MY Life Book

Softcover • ISBN-10: 0-310-70153-8
ISBN-13: 978-0-310-70153-8

(Companion Nonfiction to *Lily the Rebel*)

The It's MY Life Book is designed to help you find balance in your struggle for independence, so you can become not only your best self, but most of all your God-intended self.

....

Lights, Action, Lily! (Book Seven)

Softcover • ISBN-10: 0-310-70249-6
ISBN-13: 978-0-310-70249-8

Cast in a Shakespearean play at school by a mere fluke, Lily is immediately convinced she's destined for a career on Broadway, but finally learns through a series of entanglements that relationships are more important than a perfect performance.

The Creativity Book

Softcover • ISBN-10: 0-310-70247-X
ISBN-13: 978-0-310-70247-4
(Companion Nonfiction to *Lights, Action, Lily!*)

Discover your creativity and learn to enjoy the arts in this fun, activity-filled book written by Nancy Rue.

....

Lily Rules! (Book Eight)

Softcover • ISBN-10: 0-310-70250-X
ISBN-13: 978-0-310-70250-4

Lily is voted class president at her school, but unlike her predecessors who have been content to sail along with the title and a picture in the yearbook, Lily is out to make changes.

The Uniquely Me Book

Softcover • ISBN- 10: 0-310-70248-8
ISBN- 13: 978-0-310-70248-1
(Companion Nonfiction to *Lily Rules!*)

At some point, every girl wonders why she was born and why she's the way she is. Well, author Nancy Rue has written the perfect book designed to answer all those nagging uncertainties from a biblical perspective.

Available now at your local bookstore!

zonder**kidz**

Rough & Rugged Lily (Book Nine)

Softcover • ISBN-10: 0-310-70260-7
ISBN-13: 978-0-310-70260-3

Lily's convinced she's destined to become a great outdoorswoman, but when the Robbins family is stranded in a snowstorm on the way to a mountain cabin to celebrate Christmas, she learns the real meaning of survival and how dependent she is on the material things of life.

The Year 'Round Holiday Book

Softcover • ISBN-10: 0-310-70256-9
ISBN-13: 978-0-310-70256-6
(Companion Nonfiction to *Rough and Rugged Lily*)
The Year 'Round Holiday Book will help you celebrate traditional holidays with not only fun and pizzazz, but with deeper meaning as well.

Lily Speaks! (Book Ten)

Softcover • ISBN-10: 0-310-70262-3
ISBN-13: 978-0-310-70262-7

Lily enters the big speech contest at school and learns the up and downsides of competition through her pain and disappointment, as well as the surprise benefits, and how God heals jealousy, envy, and self-doubt.

The Values & Virtues Book

Softcover • ISBN-10: 0-310-70257-7
ISBN-13: 978-0-310-70257-3
(Companion Nonfiction to *Lily Speaks!*)
The Values & Virtues Book offers you tips and skills for improving your study habits, sportsmanship, relationships, and every area of your life.

Available now at your local bookstore!

zonder**kidz**

Horse Crazy Lily (Book Eleven)
Softcover • ISBN-10: 0-310-70263-1
ISBN-13: 978-0-310-70263-4

Lily's in love! With horses?! Back in the "saddle" for another exciting adventure, Lily's gone western and feels she's destined to be the next famous cowgirl.

The Fun-Finder Book
Softcover • ISBN-10: 0-310-70258-5
ISBN-13: 978-0-310-70258-0
(Companion Nonfiction to *Horse Crazy Lily*)

The Fun-Finder Book is designed to help you find out what you like so that you can develop your own just-for-you hobby. And if you just can't figure it out, a self-quiz helps you recognize your likes and dislikes as you discover your God-given talent.

Lily's Church Camp Adventure (Book Twelve)
Softcover • ISBN-10: 0-310-70264-X
ISBN-13: 978-0-310-70264-1

Lily learns a real lesson about the essential habits of the heart when she and the Girlz attend Camp Galilee.

The Walk-the-Walk Book
Softcover • ISBN-10: 0-310-70259-3
ISBN-13: 978-0-310-70259-7
(Companion Nonfiction to *Lily's Church Camp Adventure*)

Every young girl needs the training that develops positive and lifelong spiritual habits. Prayer, Bible study, devotion, simplicity, confession, worship, and celebration are foundational spiritual disciplines to help you "walk-the-walk."

Lily's in London?! (Book Thirteen)
Softcover • ISBN-10: 0-310-70554-1
ISBN-13: 978-0-310-70554-3

Lily's London adventures strengthen her relationship with God as she realizes, more than ever, there are many possibilities for walking her spiritual path in Christ.

Lily's Passport to Paris (Book Fourteen)
Softcover • ISBN-10: 0-310-70555-X
ISBN-13: 978-0-310-70555-0

Lily visits Paris and meets Christophe, an orphan boy at the mission where her mom is working. While helping Christophe to understand who God is, Lily finally discovers her own mission. This last book in the series also includes a letter from Nancy Rue, which tells what happens to the characters after the series ends, and introduces the character of Sophie LaCroix from the Faithgirlz! Sophie Series.

Available now at your local bookstore!

zonderkidz

Own the entire collection of Lily fiction and companion nonfiction books by Nancy Rue!

Lily Fiction Titles	Companion Nonfiction Title
Here's Lily!, Book One	The Beauty Book
Lily Robbins, M.D., Book Two	The Body Book
Lily and the Creep, Book Three	The Buddy Book
Lily's Ultimate Party, Book Four	The Best Bash Book
Ask Lily, Book Five	The Blurry Rules Book
Lily the Rebel, Book Six	The It's MY Life Book
Lights, Action, Lily!, Book Seven	The Creativity Book
Lily Rules!, Book Eight	The Uniquely Me Book
Rough & Rugged Lily, Book Nine	The Year 'Round Holiday Book
Lily Speaks!, Book Ten	The Values & Virtues Book
Horse Crazy Lily, Book Eleven	The Fun-Finder Book
Lily's Church Camp Adventure, Book Twelve	The Walk-the-Walk Book
Lily's in London?!, Book Thirteen	
Lily's Passport to Paris, Book Fourteen	

Available now at your local bookstore!

NIV Young Women of Faith Bible

General Editor: Susie Shellenberger

Hardcover • ISBN-10: 0-310-91394-2
ISBN-13: 978-0-310-91394-8

Softcover • ISBN-10: 0-310-70278-X
ISBN-13: 978-0-310-70278-8

Now there is a study Bible designed especially for
girls ages 8 to 12. Created to develop a habit of studying God's
Word in young girls, the *NIV Young Women of Faith Bible* is full of
cool, fun to read in-text features that are not only interesting, but
provide insight. It has 52 weekly studies thematically tied to the
NIV Women of Faith Study Bible to encourage a special time of
study for mothers and daughters to share in God's Word.

Available now at your local bookstore!

zonder**kidz**.

We want to hear from you. Please send your comments
about this book to us in care of zreview@zondervan.com. Thank you.

Grand Rapids, MI 49530
www.zonderkidz.com

ZONDERVAN.com/
AUTHORTRACKER
follow your favorite authors